D

LOVE IS A STRANGER

This Large Print edition is published by G.K. Hall & Co., USA and by Chivers Press, England.

Published in 2001 in the U.S. by arrangement with Golden West Literary Agency.

Published in 2001 in the U.K. by arrangement with the author.

U.S. Softcover   0-7838-9637-9   (Paperback Series Edition)
U.K. Hardcover   0-7540-4766-0   (Chivers Large Print)

The text of this Large Print edition is unabridged.
Other aspects of the book may vary from the original edition.

Set in 16 pt. Plantin by PerfecType.

Printed in the United States on permanent paper.

British Library Cataloguing in Publication Data available

Library of Congress Cataloging-in-Publication Data

Gordon, Angela, 1916–
    Love is a stranger / by Angela Gordon.
        p.   cm.
    ISBN 0-7838-9637-9 (lg. print : sc : alk. paper)
        1. New England — Fiction. 2. Large type books. I. Title.
PS3566.A34 L689 2001
813′.54—dc21   2001039764

LOVE IS A STRANGER

Angela Gordon

G.K. Hall & Co. • Chivers Press
Waterville, Maine USA • Bath, England

LOVE IS A
STRANGER

Chapter One

Old John Richards said, "What difference does it make?" to Lynne Weatherby, using a tone of voice that hinted at temper. He'd been fired a half hour earlier so he had no scruples about what he said now. "Mister Weatherby, you aren't going to live that boy's life."

Afterwards the silence drew out thin and fragile between them. Neither was a young man but age made no affinity. It couldn't have; there was something like thirteen million dollars between them. Lynne Weatherby's thirteen million. John Richards was only a yardman who had, up until he'd neglected to report Andrew Weatherby's departure, been gardener for the Weatherby estate. Now he was just another old man without a job. Worse; he was an old ex-yardman who'd just spoken up to Lynne Weatherby, Board Chairman of the E. I. Letours Corporation, Member of the Board of Union Affiliates Incorporated and a Director of the York and Westchester Trust and Savings Bank. There was no chance of John

Richards getting another job within a hundred miles of Carleton if Lynne Weatherby wished to see to that.

"Well," old John said, squinting a battered, wrinkled and tough-cast eye towards the summertime sun. "It's close to quitting time anyway, I reckon." He turned, dropped his head, squared wide, rawboned old shoulders and began to remove his leather gloves as he gazed at Lynne Weatherby. He was glinting a sardonic smile.

"I'm sorry. Not for what I told you, Mister Weatherby, but for causin' you the worry."

"You let him drive out on purpose, John," said Weatherby, levelling a keen, clear and dagger-like stare. "Don't lie to me."

Old John's smile was gone in a twinkling. "Mister Weatherby I don't lie to *no*body. I don't have to. You're plumb right; I made no move to stop the boy. I couldn't have anyway. Maybe twenty-thirty years ago . . . but he's big as a horse, strong as a bull . . . and I'm a mite slow lately."

"Deliberately, John. . . . You knew my orders!"

"Yes sir, I sure did know 'em, and yes sir, I deliberately let him drive off without telling you."

"So you're fired!"

Old John was over the numbness by now so he nodded. "All right, Mister Weatherby. I'm fired. Well; I had a job before I come here and I reckon I'll have another one after I leave here. Still and all — I'm sorry to be the cause of your misery,

fired or not. I've never been a one to like seeing folks in misery."

Lynne Weatherby was lean, grey as a wolf, tough-jawed and icy-eyed. Andrew was his only son — what John had once called a "catch colt". He came very late in his father's life. He was the only son too. In fact, since Alice Weatherby had passed on two years earlier, Andrew was all the family Lynne had on earth.

That they differed was no secret. Who would expect a lad of twenty and a man of sixty or better to see eye to eye about anything? As John told Rachel Moody the cook, "As well put a Texan and an Apache in the same tent." The simile was lost; Rachel had been born and reared not fifty miles from Carleton; all she knew and cared to know was New England. Furthermore she'd always been about half afraid of John Richards. She'd said often enough it was a pure mystery to her why as polished a man as Mister Weatherby would ever have tolerated John Richards who was by his own admission nothing but an old broken down cowboy, wild-horse runner and dissolute border ruffian from the Southwest.

Lynne Weatherby turned away, his shoulders squared, his stride stiff, his entire posture exuding outrage. John stood near the rose-tree and watched. "Sure a sad thing," he told the rose-tree, "to see a man his age at odd with his only child. But damn it all the boy's got his rights too. At twenty I'd married me two squaws and that little Mex dancer at Carlsbad. Why hells bells,

Andy's bigger'n I was them days too; what's his pappy thinkin' of trying to keep him down like this?"

Old John knew perfectly well what Lynne Weatherby was thinking of, but he'd also seen Martha O'Toole three or four times himself and what Lynne Weatherby thought was the farthest thing from old John's mind. Whoever heard of being against anyone — *especially* a girl like *that* — just because her father was a lobster fisherman who drank a little, had nothing — including credit — and was pretty generally looked down upon around Carleton?

If a man never forked a good horse until he knew who its pappy had been, he'd more'n likely spend all his time afoot. That was John's allegorical summary of such pure nonsense as he turned towards the three-room cottage to gather his things.

Now if Andy'd been twelve or thirteen maybe it would have been different, John told himself as he ambled along. Twenty is pretty well grown up. There's just not too much more that could happen to a feller — except getting old of course — after he'd reached twenty.

And as for running off to see Martha O'Toole — well — it was that time of year; even Yankee New Englanders knew the sap was running strong in springtime.

John entered the cottage, looked around — then it hit him. He went to the rocker near the window and dropped down. This was the only

real home he'd ever had. *Real* home.

Now it was no longer his.

Thirty, forty years back he'd have laughed in Lynne Weatherby's face, saddled up and loped on. Well; there was no place left to lope to, he thought sitting in the rocker, and nothing to lope *on*.

Odd how everything that's so cussed solid in a man's young years all of a sudden just plain isn't there any more at all. None of it; friends, towns, places, things. . . .

"John?"

He looked at the shadow approaching his doorway from across the yard and called back, "Come on in, Harry."

"Rachel sent down some boiled lobster."

Harry's last name was Vichter. It was pronounced like Victor. He had once told old John the reason he'd applied for the job as butler-chauffeur with Weatherby was because as a hack and truck driver in New York City he found that after he turned forty-five his reflexes were not good enough. He'd been with the Weatherbys almost five years and while he and John really had very little in common — they barely even spoke the same language as a matter of fact, Harry being a New Yorker, John Texan — they nevertheless got on very well.

"Listen," said Harry, who prefaced almost everything he said with that word. "Listen, John; Rachel heard the Old Man fire you. She come and told me."

11

Harry put the plate of lobster on a table and neither of them heeded it. John began rocking; he screwed up his leathery face into a grin. "I came here with a blanket on m'back, Harry, I'll leave the same way. Don't worry none."

"Yeah sure," muttered Harry glancing up towards the large, very handsome fieldstone house. "Listen; a good yardman shouldn't have too much trouble. . . . Of course if old Weatherby blackballs you. . . ."

"Awww; he wouldn't do a thing like that. He's just a little sore. Harry, it was time I was moving on anyway. Hell. A man sets on one roost too long he commences to get barn sour."

"Huh?"

"Well; he gets like an old horse that don't want to leave the barn where he's fed and bedded down."

"Oh. Well — yeah. Listen; John, you need any cash?"

Old John was embarrassed. So was Harry Vichter but he showed it less. "Hell no. I got money." John puckered his steady, small blue eyes. "But you know what I'd like to do before I pull the picket pin? I'd like to go over yonder, knock on the front door an' when Weatherby opened it — wham! — right in the snoot."

Harry looked shaken. He'd known John Richards several years and he still hadn't been able to make up his mind whether a lot that John said was myth or pure madness. He'd once told Rachel there just was no way to be sure whether

a Texan was wind or fact.

He now said, "He'd have you in jail so quick you'd never know how it happened."

"Naw," John disagreed. "Not when *I* hit him 'cause he wouldn't even wake up until I was over into the next county."

"Of course it's bad to be fired, John, but —"

"Naw, Harry. That's not why I'd like to bust him one. It's because he needs his brains shaken up a mite. He treats Andy like he was ten years old." The small blue eyes lifted again to Vichter's face. They were shrewd and calculating. "You know what, Harry? That damned old man's *forcin'* the kid to buck him. He's making Andy do everything wrong just by saying 'No' to him all the time. I saw that when I first come here, when Andy used to come out where I was working and we'd talk. Old Weatherby may be a multi-millionaire; he may be as smart as a whip on finance, but Harry he's the dumbest damned fool I ever saw about folks. His own folks included. *That's* why I'd like to bust him in the mouth."

Harry didn't even like the sound of this kind of talk. "Listen; hitting someone don't change their mind, John. Besides, you're too old. And so is Weatherby. You might break something in him. Then where'd you be?"

John's long lips parted revealing straight, worn teeth. "Oh don't fret, son, I'm not going to *do* it. I just said I'd like to do it."

"John; you want a drink? I got some Southern

13

Comfort over in my cottage. Listen; suppose I go get it?"

"That'd be right neighbourly of you, Harry," replied the older man, and whipped up out of his chair. "I'll wait for you out on the porch."

Old John was whipcord-tough and ramrod-straight. He didn't weigh as much as square-hewn Harry Vichter but he was taller and although some older, moved with more grace and poise.

Harry ducked out into the early evening and headed for one of the other cottages where the estate help resided. John went out too but stopped on his little porch. It was fragrant out there, the sun was dropping away, crickets chirped and a gull soaring inland mewed.

He'd never expected to like this Yankee country one bit. In fact he'd only taken Weatherby's job to get enough grubstake to get back to the border country. He'd bought three books on flowers and gardening and had kept out of everyone's way the first month until he could learn enough to fool folks into thinking he really was a yard-man.

He'd fooled them. He'd also fooled himself. He'd come to enjoy working the grounds, but then he'd always liked using his hands and being out of doors. Finally, he and Andrew Weatherby had got to be close, so the whole thing had drifted on until today, and otherwise the Lord only knew when it would've ended — maybe never because the longer old John had stayed the

less he remembered that other place in his heart.

He said aloud to himself in the lonely gloaming, "Well, you consarned old fool, you knew when you commenced makin' the boy over you were headin' for trouble. You can't make 'em independent and not have to clash with their folks because of it." He looked up where golden lamplight shone from the big fieldstone house, his jaw squared, his little blue eyes hard as stone. "All right Weatherby you old fossil; let's you *un*-make him. Leastways now he's his own man. Let's see you *un*-do that!"

Chapter Two

Michael O'Toole was a slight man of about five feet and nine inches. He didn't weigh over one hundred and fifty pounds and he didn't particularly resemble an Irishman; he was dark. His hair was black, his eyes dark, his skin swarthy. Except for the even features he might have been some kind of Latin. Also except for his love of the spirits too; in that regard he was a true son of the Auld Sod.

It was said O'Toole could drink more, show it less, fish better and pay slower than anyone in Carleton.

His residence on a tributary creek leading out into Pawtucket River wasn't on stilts like some shacks were down there in the disreputable part of town, but it had never been painted, the roofline had a definite sway, and with lobster traps hanging upon the outside walls it looked less like a home than most.

Mike's daughter was as good a fisherman as he was, folks said, but then there would be a good reason for that; Martha had quit school before graduating. Both she and her father pretended it was because she'd learned all high school had to offer. Both knew differently; she'd quit because her spirit had shrivelled those last two years. She was as pretty in her dark way — prettier in fact which may have been part of the trouble — than any of the other girls from town, but they'd dressed better, had money to spend, and finally, the things they said about Martha O'Toole sent the boys down to the creek to see if it was true.

It wasn't, but that didn't alleviate the pain any so Martha had quit school in her junior year and had become her father's right hand. When he'd get too drunk she'd tend the traps. When he'd be too sick after being too drunk, she'd load up the lobsters, drive up through town and sell them.

Martha wasn't a very big girl; maybe about five feet two inches tall, but she was brown as a berry, muscular and in her dark gypsy way, as pretty as anything a man would ever see, anywhere.

She had the Irish laughter, the wise and know-ing eyes, the quick compassion and the high and dark arched brows that could descend like night when she was displeased, which she was when Andrew Weatherby left his convertible near the trees and came stalking round front where she was mooring the boat. She looked a sight. Being out in the boat most of the day hardly helped a girl qualify for much; she always tried to be neat and squeaky-clean when he came along. This time, with no advance warning, she was annoyed.

But she said nothing as he helped her loop the line, toss out the box-traps, set the oars, because his face was dogged, his eyes stormy and hard. Afterwards, wiping their hands on the same filthy rag, he said, "You didn't expect me."

She hadn't, of course, but then he hadn't asked it as a question either, so all she said was, "You're mad, Andy. Paw's gone up to town. Help me get supper," and started to turn away. He caught her arm roughly wheeling her back around.

"I told my father I was going to marry you."

She was like stone, black eyes rummaging his face. "And he said you weren't."

Andrew's lips curled — downwards. "That's not all he said."

"You argued?"

"Not actually. I just left."

She kept searching, her brilliant black gaze turning troubled. "Andy . . . ?"

"No! You said you loved me, Marty."

"I *do*. And you *know* I do."

He dropped his hand from her arm. His handsome face softened away from its hardness slowly. Then he smiled. "Well; at least *that's* still the same, Marty," he murmured, looking straight down into her face. "Everything else sure is going to pot — but at least I've still got that."

"You'll always have that," she said softly, breasts rising and falling a little quicker. "Whether we're ever married or not, Andy."

"Whether . . . ?"

"I'm afraid of him."

Andrew took her hands, squeezed and said, "I am too, but not in the same way. We'll get married all right. The day you say you're ready. He can't stop *that*."

"Then what?" she asked soberly. "You come down here and tend lobster traps? Andy you know — "

"We talked that all out. No. We'll go somewhere else and I'll go to work." He turned her, guiding her towards the old shack. "Everyone else does it, and I'm at least educated as an engineer whether I've ever been one or not."

She didn't argue but as they passed inside and she flicked on the lights she look long at him. There was doubt and fear in her glance.

"He had John watching to see I didn't leave tonight, Marty."

"Did John try to stop you?"

Andrew soft-smiled. "You know better than that. Old John and I are pardners."

"Then he'll be angry with John."

"He'll get over it. He always does if he's given enough time."

"But one of these times. . . ."

"Don't worry, love. He'd probably never admit it but he thinks the world of old John." Andrew laughed. "It's odd actually; they are as un-alike as any two men you've ever seen. But dad listens when John speaks. Know what I think it is? In one of the psychology classes I took at college we learned about sedentary people being fascinated by — "

"This isn't a college class," she said sharply as he came forth from the back of the house where she'd left a door open as she'd scrubbed. Heading now for the stove she said, "Don't forget I've talked to your father too, Andy, and he made me feel all shrivelled up inside. Whether he liked John or not — he's still my biggest enemy. . . . Unless it's something else."

She got very busy by the stove. He dropped onto a chair and watched her. From front or rear she was supple, muscular, perfectly co-ordinated and voluptuous. He was twenty years old, burly and healthy. He had to look elsewhere to keep the train of thought when he said, "What? Honey you don't have any enemies. You've got me." His blue eyes twinkled ironically. "Of course that practically insures you'll be talked about. Everyone I've ever gone with got talked about."

"That's natural. Your father's the richest man in town. That's not what I was thinking about, Andy."

"What then?"

"Would you like some coffee?"

"Later. What were you thinking about?"

She turned. "You and me. We're healthy and in love. But there's an awful lot more to it than that."

He nodded, hunching thick shoulders forward as he looked straight at her. "I know that. I'm prepared."

"For — *all* of it? We can get married. I suppose he can't really do too much about that. But lately

I've been trying to see into our future, Andy. I'm Mike O'Toole's girl from down in shantytown."

He was unmoved. "All right. What of it? I'm not exactly a simpleton, Marty. I've done my share of soul-searching too. You're thinking you won't know which fork to use or how to talk or what to say, or even how to dress." His tone was ruthless, his expression hard as iron. It made him resemble his father. But the words were sensible; they sounded almost as earthly as the words of old John Richards.

"You know what *really* matters? That you're honest, truthful, decent. That you always will be. That you'll try as hard as I will. *That's* what matters."

She blinked several times, rapidly and turned back.

"Do you know who you sounded like just now, Andy?"

"I know. What difference does that make. It's the truth isn't it?"

"I — think so. I — hope it is."

He arose moving towards her but she quickly thrust a pen into his hand saying, "Get the shellfish I left in the big trap. The water'll be boiling in a minute."

He looked at the pan he was holding, looked at her averted profile, then stalked back outside. The moment he was gone she ran into her tiny bedroom, groped for a fresh handkerchief and sobbed into it. She'd never thought love would come like this; she'd read romance magazines in the summer twilight down where the creek lapped a sandy shore, and in those stories love had come gently, tenderly.

This — this was a fight. This wasn't *ever* going to be a tender nor a gentle love. At least not for as long as she could foresee.

She regained control, washed her face in cold water and went back to the stove making herself breathe deeply in and out, which was the only way she knew to keep tears back. She also concentrated on other things. The disappointingly small catch today, the note her father had left saying he'd gone up to see about selling the catch — which she knew was only an excuse — and the fact that if anyone ever saw her alone in the shack with Andrew Weatherby terrible things would be said throughout town.

When he returned the water was boiling. He looked inquiringly and she nodded so he dropped the lobsters in. That was something she'd never got used to, seeing their violent brief spasms. But her father said there was no other way, and she turned to take the pan from Andy so it was over before she had to look the second time.

Andy got himself a glass of water, leaned alongside her making it seem the most natural thing in the world for them to be like this. She felt her inner response throughout every muscle and nerve to his closeness. She also knew this was their biggest private danger — they were both young and very much alive.

She made the coffee and moved away to set the

table. "Dad's not likely to be back for supper," she stated matter-of-factly, "but I'll set his place anyway." It made things seem more proper that way to her.

Andy finished his water, watched her a moment then said, "I'll get another argument when I go home tonight." He set the glass aside. "Marty . . . ?"

She turned, lifting dark eyes. His tone had changed.

"Suppose we went uptown and got married tonight — after dinner."

She turned back to finish setting the table as though he'd said the most natural thing in the world — like it might rain or there was a full moon or he'd heard her father's car coming.

"Marty . . . ?"

"I heard you."

"Well . . . ?"

She very carefully put aside the silverware, went straight up to him and raised both arms. There was a bright shininess to her dark gaze. He caught her close with young-cub roughness and nearly squeezed the breath out of her. Then he dropped his head straight down, sought her lips and bore down with all the fierce demands of youth.

She met his passion with an equal passion. She held him round the shoulder with muscles bunched and steely; felt the searing fire of his want and only tried to twist away when she heard the car outside.

They stepped clear looking guilty. She whipped back to finish at the table while he drew forth a white handkerchief and vigorously scrubbed his lips.

Mike O'Toole came in with a raffish grin and a breath that reached as far as where Andrew stood. But he wasn't drunk, simply in very high spirits.

"I thought you might be down here," he said to Andrew by way of greeting. "I heard up at — the store — there'd been a blowup at your place."

Both of them looked round. Andrew said, slowly, "A — blowup . . . ?"

"Aye, son. Your father fired old John Richards."

While Mike shed his thin coat and carefully placed several packages upon the sideboard Martha and Andrew eyed him.

"Well," said Mike cheerily, turning to cock a knowing eye at them, "I knew it'd end about like this, an' if you two didn't it's only because you're young yet. After all, Mister Weatherby isn't the kind t'take lightly to havin' his boy influenced by someone like old John Richards."

Mike stabbed a playful finger towards Andrew. "But I'd have t'also say John Richards is a smart man in his way. He'd teach youngsters to stand and give as good as they take."

Andrew straightened up, shot Martha a look and said, "I'll go home now, Marty. You understand."

She nodded clenching both hands around a

pair of water glasses. "Of course. Andy . . . ? If John needs a place to stay. . . ."

Andrew nodded, ducked around chuckling Mike O'Toole and ran out into the settling night.

Chapter Three

Rachel Moody had survived the cut-back in domestic help after Mrs. Weatherby had died and Mr. Weatherby began to entertain less, stay at home more, because she'd been with the family longest, but also because she knew exactly what foods, and how to prepare them, Lynne Weatherby could eat. There were definitely some things he could not and would not eat.

Rachel was short and dumpy and durable. No one, including Rachel, could remember the last time she'd been ill. She was, as Mrs. Weatherby had often said, the most thoroughly predictable and dependable person on earth.

Rachel had been almost an aunt to Andrew while he'd been growing up. A wise old aunt for all her priggish New England ways, so when Andrew returned from the O'Toole place after flinging out of the house earlier, Rachel knew what was going to happen. It did. It happened in the formal sitting-room where she could hear every word of it. It began with Andrew stepping in and saying to his father in a very normal tone of voice: "Did you fire John Richards?"

Lynne Weatherby sitting with his back to the room, his face to a cold and black fireplace upon the mantel of which stood a gold-framed picture of his wife, had answered back without looking round.

"I did."

"Because I drove out tonight?"

"Yes. But not entirely for that."

"Not because he wasn't a good yardman, father, nor because he lied or stole like others have done."

"Andrew. . . ." The elder Weatherby heaved round on the sofa. He had a half-emptied highball glass in his hand. "I've been sitting here thinking. Of course you're the only heir I have. That simply means you'll benefit from my estate. Anyway, that's how things were set up through the attorney years ago and I wouldn't change that. But. . . ." The older man got up, now, stepped to the cold fireplace and put his back to it, still holding the half empty highball glass and gazing across the formally elaborate room towards his burly son. "But. . . . I'm going to give you an ultimatum. The next time you walk away from me as you did tonight and fling out of this house — you will not be allowed back."

Rachel was horrified. She stood like a statue in the butler's pantry.

Andrew's retort was slow coming. The voice was pitched to a rough lowness when he said,

27

"Do you know what you can do with your estate?"

"Andrew you'd better be careful!"

Rachel gripped the edge of a cold tabletop. She wanted to run yet she couldn't.

"Dad; the hell with your estate."

"I warned you, Andrew. . . ."

"I asked Martha O'Toole to marry me tonight. That's exactly what I'm going to do, too, marry her. As for what your attorneys have worked up — don't do me any favours. Dad I'm not able to compromise very well. I suppose I get that from you. But if I can't have Marty *and* my home, then I'll take Marty and make a home of my own."

"You ridiculous pup," said Lynne Weatherby in deep scorn. "Do you imagine I've tried to prevent that marriage because I have anything against the *girl?* You're too young and stupid to understand. It's not the girl — it's what she represents. She'd never be able to make the climb, boy. Believe me I know what I'm saying; she'd embarrass you. Not too much at first — there'd be the physical rewards to compensate — but later on, after four or five years . . . and it would get steadily more unbearable."

"We've talked about that."

"I'm sure you have," said the older man, raised and emptied his highball glass. "I'm sure you've talked of a lot of things. But what kind of a conclusion can someone come to who's never earned a cent in his life, who's never had to make a decision that didn't involve his own con-

28

founded indulgence . . . ?"

Rachel heard Weatherby put down the emptied glass, hard. She heard Andrew's weight shift as though he might be stalking his father. Her heart nearly stopped. Then she heard the son's voice again.

"Maybe not a *right* decision every time like a banker, Dad, but a damned sight more humane one. What kind of a yellowbelly would fire John Richards simply because he was so mad at his son he had to hurt someone, and with the son out of reach old John was handiest?"

". . . Andrew; you've said enough."

"No I haven't. I've got one more thing to say. *I'm glad mother is dead!*"

Rachel reeled against the pantry table, one hand flying to her heart.

"It would have been hell on her to be in the middle, Dad, and that's where she'd have been tonight. But at least she didn't try to keep me in knee-pants after I outgrew them."

Rachel heard Lynne Weatherby stride away from the fireplace. She heard ice tinkle into a glass and the hiss of a soda-water bottle. Mister Weatherby was fixing himself another highball — "nightcap" as he called them. That was unusual; in all the years she'd been with them she'd only known this to happen twice before. Once, when the United States declared war on Germany and again when the Japanese attacked Pearl Harbour.

"All right, son," came the clipped, strong voice, sounding battered and weary. "All right.

There is no way to argue without hurting and being hurt, so I'm sorry for all that's been said here tonight. Now go upstairs, pack what you'll need and leave. There is still something like fifteen hundred dollars in your college cheque fund — use it sparingly because from tonight on, you and I are related by blood but in no other way. Good luck."

It was coolly said right down to the "good luck." Rachel knew that tone. She could even imagine Lynne Weatherby's erect, grey and stone-faced stance. He might even melodramatically lift the highball glass in salute. But no, Rachel knew better; he wasn't a dramatic type man, he was a New Englander, flinty, unrelenting, hard and *right*. He'd scorn melodramatics.

The last thing Andrew said was, "Thanks," then Rachel heard him heading up the stairs to his room taking them two at a time.

Finally, she returned to the kitchen, set the tea water to boil, got a cup, saucer and spoon, went to the table and sat. Now the house was quiet as a tomb. She bit her lip. What a terrible thing for a child to say about his mother, even if he hadn't meant it as it had initially sounded.

These things just didn't happen in New England. In places such as California, yes, but not in New England. And Mister Weatherby. . . . She got the water, steeped the tea, poured in milk and stirred. Mister Weatherby hadn't handled the boy well at all.

She was finishing the tea when he walked into

the kitchen holding his empty highball glass and looking part lost, part ill. She didn't give him a chance. Sitting primly erect Rachel swept up one hand to make certain her greying hair was perfectly in place, then fired her blunt salvo.

"I'd like my time tonight if it pleases you, sir."

He turned very slowly to stare. She had to face those commanding blue eyes head-on but she was descended from Yankee sea captains too, so she gave look for look without so much blinking.

"Your time — Rachel? Whatever for?"

"Mister Weatherby; I was in the pantry. I didn't mean to be, but I heard what you told Andrew."

"Oh. And you think I'm wrong?"

"Just my time, please, Mr. Weatherby."

He shook out of the trauma, crossed over and eased down opposite her at the kitchen table. "Rachel; the boy defied me. He's deliberately permitted himself to become infatuated with that O'Toole girl. I tell you — and of all people *you* ought to know it's true — he's only making grief for himself. Lord! All I'm trying to do is save him."

Rachel sat silently erect her rounded jaw doggedly set. "Mister Weatherby it's not my lot to argue, but I've my own set of rules, so if you'll be kind enough — "

"*No!*" Lynne Weatherby jack-knifed up off the chair, slammed the highball glass atop the table and left it there as he stepped back. A disinterested spectator might have been able to compare him to a gladiator whose allies had left him, back

31

to the wall, fighting alone. "I'll not pay you off, Rachel. And you're perfectly correct — none of what has happened is any of your affair."

She had her answer ready. She delivered it as any other Yankee would have; without raising her voice but with a look of dark fire in her flinty eyes too. "I'm not taking issue — at least I'm not *outwardly* taking sides, Mister Weatherby. As you say, it's none of my affair. But all the same I'm a free agent, and free agents have a right to work — and *not* work — where they wish. If you'll not make out the cheque, I'll call round for it later."

She stood up to her full, round height and was a head and a half shorter than Lynne Weatherby, but her resolve made her just as determined and therefore just as tall.

"If you'll excuse me," she snapped, and stepped past him bound for her private quarters off the kitchen.

Lynne Weatherby turned to watch Rachel disappear into her quarters, then started out of the kitchen, thought of something, went back after his highball glass and took it along as he returned to the formal sitting-room. But he couldn't find comfort there so went and stood at the base of the stairs listening; there wasn't a sound from Andrew's room. He didn't believe the boy could have packed and left so quickly, so he climbed up to see.

There was no sign of his son and although a closet door stood ajar, he could see the suits and jackets hanging inside. He went to a window and looked down towards the great curving driveway. Andrew's convertible was still out there, creamy in the summertime moonlight. He turned a little gaze over where the cottages were and saw the lights blazing in Richard's bungalow. His hand whitened at the knuckles around the highball glass. He turned and marched back downstairs and into his oak-panelled study. He couldn't very well storm over and interrupt whatever old John and his son were saying although he'd have liked to. He'd wait until Andrew left then have Vichter drive old John off the place — take him somewhere in town for the night — get him off the estate.

There were four pictures on the large mahogany desk. Two were of the family when he and Alice had been younger, when Andrew had been quite small. Another picture was of Andrew beside his first automobile — a small, ugly little bug of a car. The other photograph was of Alice, dead two years now.

Lynne sat at the desk, leaned back still holding his empty glass, and gazed at the little smile on his wife's face.

"... *It would have been hell on her to be in the middle, Dad. ...*"

He arose somewhat quickly and went back out to the formal sitting-room and made himself another highball. His third one.

The house creaked as it always did on hot summer nights. Stone walls three feet thick were impervious but interior woodwork and roof-rafters weren't. When he'd first brought Alice here she'd said it was more like a mausoleum than a home, and had at once set about making it a credit to the twentieth century rather than a place locally noted for the fact that once Benedict Arnold had lain in it with a crushed right foot when a horse had fallen on him in a skirmish with the British.

The third highball didn't make Lynne Weatherby drunk. He was a rock-ribbed New Englander; whether they believed in the use of liquor or not — and most did in their homes while denouncing it outside their homes — it took a good deal to make a New Englander drunk. Moreover, he had a taste of gall and ashes in his gullet which prevented him from feeling anything, really, except a kind of emptiness; a kind of hollow misery that beat in his temples after he'd downed the third whiskey and water.

Once, he'd heard John Richards say that after three years amongst Yankees he finally knew why they'd won the Civil War. The exact words had stuck in Lynne Weatherby's head.

"You can kill 'em but you sure as hell cain't *change* 'em!"

He pushed the glass away, went to sit before the cold, cheerless fireplace again, and there he fell sound asleep.

Chapter Four

Harry Vichter drove John Richards into Carleton and left him. Harry was troubled. Neither of them knew Rachel had quit or their sense of crisis would have been heightened. Nonetheless Harry told John he'd come back and see him within a day or two, when he got a chance to slip away with one of the Weatherby cars.

The town wasn't much. That is it wasn't very large. It almost fit the category of a village, but it had one distinction. The Weatherby estate wasn't the only residence of wealthy people. For many years, in fact since before the turn of the century, New Yorkers had been coming up to Carleton. At first there'd been what in those days was called a "spa." None of the natives now used the word at all, and even when they had used it hadn't been sure of its meaning except that it sounded European and therefore had to be elegant. Later, folks said Carleton was a "wonderful watering place." There was an old bath-house with mud-baths and heated, mineral-water pools, but that withered between the World Wars. Later, mon-eyed people kept estates at Carleton because it was handy to commuter trains and because it was peaceful.

It was also, John Richards had once observed, "colder'n Billy-be-damned" in wintertime. All New England was. The old Currier and Ives lith-ographs showing sleighs and prancing horses, people wrapped in robes and ice-skating on the ponds were very nostalgic, but like the beauty on the outside of Christmas cards, they only showed what people liked to see, not what they actually *felt*, standing hock-deep in snow.

But a New England summertime was like nothing on earth unless perhaps it was an Old England summertime. That's what brought wealthy families and what kept them around Carleton. They'd flee to Florida in winter-time and return after the last frost. It made good con-ditions. Carleton's canny Yankee natives kept their brick buildings scrubbed, their old-fashioned white wainscotings gleaming, their shop-fronts quaint with brass and copper. People — especially wealthy people — stayed in a place that was quaint. They also spent money there.

Of course there was shantytown, but every vil-lage on earth had its poor quarter. Carleton had, years back, stabilized and camouflaged the houses down along the tributary creek. Poplars grew abundantly down there, multiflora roses added still another screen. Restrictions kept people like Michael O'Toole from moving into better housing the same as it kept him from adding on to what he already had. Shantytown, folks said, was a blight but after all those *were* human beings down there so no one would discriminate against them.

The trouble with that outlook was that those giant sentinel poplars and the thorned multiflora bushes were simply a landscaped variety of barbed wire. People from shantytown were different.

Old John went down there the day after he'd left the Weatherby estate and had a nip with Mike O'Toole who was friendly and generous, among other things, but when John, long scrawny legs folded under him, said "I expect it's mostly my fault, the lad getting into trouble and all," Mike shot him a quick look and replied, "No; I don't see as you hardly figure in it at all. The boy's in love with my girl. That's about all there is to it. If Mister Weatherby's going to be difficult. . . ." Mike heaved a big shrug, sipped his watered whiskey and glanced down where his boat was tied. "They'll get married anyway. And the boy's still his papa's heir." The little sly eyes turned back. "Nothing's going to change that."

Old John looked straight at O'Toole, surprised. He kept studying him. Finally, setting aside the cup in his hand he levered himself up into a standing position. Over at the house there was no sign of Martha.

"Well," he drawled, "I'd best be hikin' back. Just thought I'd drop by and visit for a spell."

"Sure," said O'Toole without arising. "Come by any time, Mist' Richards."

When John reached the end of town where his hotel stood — a very inexpensive place, used frequently by second- and third-rate salesmen — he saw Martha getting into her father's old car.

Actually it wasn't a car although at one time it had been. Mike had cut the body off just behind the front seat. Where the rear seat and half the body had once been he'd bolted on some heavy timbers making a truck-of-sorts of the auto. For his purpose it was better that way. Also, in the summertime it wasn't difficult to guess what Mike's business was; old John caught the smell of fish before he'd even come close.

Martha saw him and turned to watch his approach. She smiled, a trifle sadly, and said, "I'm awfully sorry about what happened, Mister Richards."

He tucked up the corners of his mouth. "Nothing to fret over girl. I been workin' out there so long, with no place to go and nothing to do, that I'm enjoyin' the vacation."

"Well. . . ." she fiddled with the gear-shift lever.

John leaned upon the door studying her golden colouring and fine, even features. By grabs, up close she was even prettier; he'd have given a lot right then to have been a young buck of forty again.

"Seen Andy yet today?" he asked.

She shook her head. "He's gone to New York."

John was surprised. "New York? What in tarnation for?"

"To try and find work."

"Well; what's the matter with workin' right here in Carleton?"

"He says it wouldn't work out. In the first place no one would hire him. They'd know who he was and be afraid to. In the second place there's no work for engineers around here."

"Well," spluttered old John. "But New York. Girl; that's too far off."

Her soft mouth drooped and long black lashes batted swiftly as she said, "If he can find something . . . then we'll be married and I'll go down there with him."

John almost groaned. He'd been to New York City twice in the past four years. It was the most god-awful bewildering place he'd ever seen in his lifetime. It sort of sneaked up and grabbed a man round the throat, making him feel cooped in and strangling.

"That's no place for young folks to set up housekeeping, Martha-girl. Good Lord A'mighty you dassn't even breathe the air, and there's nothing but smoke and soot and cement. Young love needs green grass and blue skies. Take old John Richards' word for that."

"Yes but there's nothing else we can do, Mister Richards." The black, liquid eyes raised and jumped hopelessly from store-front to store-front. "There's nothing in Carleton for young people. You can see that, can't you?"

Whether old John saw that or not he wasn't going to admit it. "Well," he said, groping his way. "Tell you what; when he comes home tonight send him down to my room at the hotel — the place yonder with the dirty curtains upstairs. We'll talk a little."

She nodded politely and drove off. John stepped back on the pavement and watched the exhaust smoke, finally feeling the first real anger he'd ever felt against Lynne Weatherby. In a way he was angry with himself too; he felt, regardless of whatever Mike O'Toole had said, that he was largely at fault for this whole mess.

"Richards."

He turned, at once recognizing the short, dumpy figure of Rachel Moody. He smiled downward. He'd always known she hadn't much cared for him. He didn't quite understand why except that he called her a Yankee, but he liked to tease her so he said, "Miz' Moody, I do declare you keep lookin' younger and more pert every time I see you."

She blushed as she always did but this time she couldn't turn and flee to the house. She didn't look like she'd have done it anyway; she stood there square and solid looking straight up into his little blue eyes.

"I suppose you've heard I quit last night, Mister Richards."

He hadn't heard and the shock sobered him at once. "You — done quit Mister Weatherby?"

"Last night."

"Well I'll be . . . what for, Miz' Moody?"

"You ought to know, you've been egging the boy on ever since you came here; teaching him to stand up to others. He and his father had a — discussion — when he got back last night. But you'd know about that since he went down to your bungalow."

"Well yes'm, he told me about that. Only I still don't see what it's got to do with you quittin'."

"I heard it, Mister Richards. I was in the pantry and heard every word of it. I'll not work for a man who can't handle his children any better than Mister Weatherby did last night."

"You told old Weatherby that?"

Rachel sniffed. "Of course not."

"What do you mean — 'of course not'?"

"Unlike you, Mister Richards, I know my place."

John stroked his jaw saying quietly, "Oh. Well now, ma'am, just how do you reckon a man like old Weatherby's ever goin' to learn much if folks are so busy kowtowing to him they're scairt to speak their minds."

"It has nothing to do with being afraid of Mister Weatherby, Mister Richards. As for speaking one's mind — that's what you've been doing ever since you arrived on the estate, and look what it's caused!"

Old John digested that very slowly. He gave his grizzled head a little wag as though to say this conversation wasn't going anywhere because its participants were just too totally different.

"Miz' Moody; even for a *Yankee* you're cantan-kerous," he said pleasantly. "But old Weatherby's going to — "

"Stop saying 'Old Weatherby'. It's *Mister* Weatherby."

John nodded, unflustered. "*Mister* Weatherby's going to miss you more'n he'll miss the boy or me. Who'll cook for him now?"

Rachel's thin lips flattened. "Richards, you're pathetically ignorant about some things. He can have someone sent in from the village or he can telephone down to the city. That will prove the least of his troubles I can assure you."

"Naw," drawled old John. "Miz' Moody, he's not going to find another one that can cook like you do."

Rachel's plump cheeks pinked up. She looked away and shifted weight as though to move on. John was blocking her way.

"I'd bet you a dollar against a doughnut he'll come after you, Miz' Moody."

"It would do no good. I told him last night I'd not work out there."

John kept gazing at her. "By golly," he murmured, "I knew the *men* was bullheaded. . . ."

"Good day to you, Mister Richards."

"Yes'm," he said, stepping aside to avoid being struck head-on. He smiled, stepped over into store-front shade and watched the sturdy white-clad figure march on down the southward walkway.

Of course she was right about him. She'd never

much liked him and now she felt he was behind all the trouble. Well; as a matter of fact he felt he was too.

He turned and went ambling down towards his little hotel. He hadn't yet made up his mind what he'd do. Maybe go back down to Texas. Maybe seek another job around Carleton on one of the large estates. Maybe just loaf for a month or two. He had just about all the money he'd ever been paid out at Weatherby's. Like he'd said, there'd been no place to spend it. But there was more — a man old John's age had few needs and no dissipations. Once in a while a film, supper at the one cafe in town that served *chili con carne,* one or two beers.

He halted out front of the hotel and watched a shiny blue auto go by. He knew both the car and the driver. Old Weatherby and his Lincoln Continental.

John puckered up his eyes in quiet thought and watched the car stop out front of a little brick and white-woodwork building with a medical doctor's shingle over the door.

Weatherby went in. He looked a little rumpled, not at all as immaculate as he ordinarily looked. Harry Vichter had once told John that Rachel had told him Lynne Weatherby had ulcers.

John nodded to himself, turned and entered the musty, gently threadbare little lobby. If old Weatherby had a lick of sense he'd go hunt down Rachel Moody and get her back if he had to double her salary.

Climbing the stairs to his room though, John thought of Rachel's stubborn jaw. Nope; the salary wouldn't have enough to do with it. John wasn't sure exactly what it *would* take to put Lynne Weatherby's life back in proper order again. He only thought that the rich man was one of the biggest fools he'd ever known.

Chapter Five

A number like Ten Million ordinarily conveys a degree of vastness beyond comprehension. If someone had told Andrew Weatherby there were ten million people in New York City it wouldn't have surprised him at all because he'd probably heard it before; it was a very common statistic. But to imagine ten million of anything — matches, trees, dollars or people was just like saying twenty or thirty million. No one had a way of visualising ten million anythings, not even with wide-angle perception.

But when Andrew got back to the commuter station in mid-afternoon after seeing as many employment agencies and private firms as he could — with no encouragement anywhere — he began to appreciate what the number Ten Million meant. It was an un-nerving discovery because it didn't convey a staggering assortment of human beings at all; it instead conveyed the smallness, the unimportance of just *one* individual.

He'd been to New York City many times, often with his father and nearly as often alone on shopping trips. But that was a different New York. When a man seeks work he doesn't belong to that other world at all. He is a fragile, unconfident, naked human being stepping through doors onto a slave-block all day long, being viewed and questioned and rejected.

It was even worse because Andrew, despite his size, was quite young. Twice there'd been flickers of interest; he was Lynne Weatherby's son. But neither time did that, in the end, mean anything. He'd told them his father didn't even know he was looking for work, which probably meant to the cold-faced, sleek men there'd be no chance of interesting wealthy Lynne Weatherby in promotional schemes or land development.

He rode back to Carleton with sore soles and a sensation of bitter frustration. He thought that if colleges taught a course in bilking or deceiving or perhaps even outright bank robbery they'd be fitting students better for the fight to survive. Undergraduate engineers, one practical but not unkindly older man had told him, were a dime-a-dozen. They were used as chainmen for surveyors, rarely as anything more lofty.

The man advised Andrew to finish his senior year then come back. Andrew had said, "To be a surveyor's chain-man — with a degree?" The older man had acidly smiled. "Nobody starts at the top, son. Not any more. Unless of course your father wants to foot the bill."

It wasn't a very attractive picture. Andrew rode back on the commuter train sunk in gloom. He'd been offered a scholastic scholarship in a Midwestern university four months earlier, but all he'd had to do was look up the school to discover it had the Midwest championship in football to imagine what in that case "scholastic" meant.

When he arrived back in Carleton it was late afternoon. His car was still parked at the depot where he'd left it. There was a folded slip of paper wedged into the steering-wheel. His heart gave a queer little flutter as he unfolded the note. It was from Martha; she said John Richards wanted to see him later on, and told where old John was staying.

He pocketed the note, drove out to the north end of town, had a sandwich and a glass of milk at a little cafe then drove straight down to the creek through the screen of giant poplars and multiflora bushes.

Mike wasn't home but Martha was. She was finishing up the dinner dishes and heard his car. By the time he reached the clearing she was outside gazing up where the dirt road ended out back, her hair, black, curly, worn short, sleek from a quick brushing, her fresh dress crisp still from ironing, her face and bare arms golden-tan in the late-day shadows.

She watched him stride ahead and let her breath out slowly; she knew that expression. He said, "Hi," then he shook his head at her.

"Nothing. I could've got a job chaining for a sur-veyor but we couldn't have lived on what they'd pay."

She had no idea what "chaining" was but it didn't matter. She said, "Have you eaten?"

"Yes. Out at the little cafe north of town."

She knew where that was; they went there often together. She wanted to cheer him up; to make that ugly look leave his features. "Well; it's probably just as well. We had lobster again." She stepped off the rickety porch, took his hand and tugged him along towards the creek. "This is only the first day, Andy." She cocked a sideways look at him. "Don't you suppose everyone has to go through this when they first start out?"

He didn't answer. He was one of those people who took their hurts hard. He'd always been like this. Not sullen, just inclined to slip down into deep silence.

She stopped where her father's old boat gently rocked, its scarred, battered sides showing where lobster-traps had been carelessly hauled up over the wood for years. It made her feel the futility of her existence. Nothing ever changed; nothing got better. The same shack, same boat, same bleak outlook.

He said, also eyeing the boat, "Is your dad home?"

"No. Why?"

"Well; I need to work it off. If he wouldn't care maybe I could row the boat."

She agreed instantly, wishing to help him out

of his mood. She stepped in, reached to fling off the tether then balanced lightly as he also got in. The boat settled under his solid weight. She smiled as he eased down and used one oar to shove off with.

"By the time you're forty you're going to weigh a ton, Andy."

He grunted, set the locks, adjusted the oars and leaned to his work. He stopped where they entered the Pawtucket to shed his coat; it bound him across the shoulders. She sat down in the bow, legs close, elbows on her knees, watching him. He was astonishingly powerful. He was also handsome. In some ways he put her in mind of his father. He would be a very difficult person to influence, but he was fair and reasonable and honest. And he laughed with a boyish warmth that never failed to thrill her. She sighed and sat, saying nothing while he caught the rhythm of the tide and moved his body with it, making the oars rise with feathered grace, then bite in hard, sending the boat shooting upriver.

"Andy. . . . We can wait. Today's disappointments don't have to mean anything. We're young."

He looked straight at her as he leaned, then reared back against the resistance of the water against his oar-blades. He did that twice before he said anything although he kept looking straight at her.

"I've been waiting, Marty. We both have. I think I've been going about this all wrong. I shouldn't be going after the work. I should be making it come to me."

"I don't understand, Andy."

He smiled ruefully, but it nevertheless was a smile. "I don't myself, exactly, but the notion keeps coming back to me."

They weren't far from the shore. A veritable jungle of trees and undergrowth was over there. Opposite them was a sloping clearing and an elegant white-painted boat-house belonging to some big estate. Otherwise though, the land was rough and rolling and covered with undergrowth. Carleton had perhaps expanded in the past fifty or seventy-five years but it hadn't done so to the north; here, everything seemed pretty much as it must have looked to the first pioneers. Barring, of course, those brushed-off places where big estates were.

The Pawtucket was at times a wilful river, but not around Carleton where the channel ran nearly straight and amply wide to accommodate floodtides. Down there it was almost sluggish, particularly in the summertime. But it also had enough little backwater eddies where there was no movement to encourage mosquitoes. They at times made boating almost impossible. Or had, in years past. Now, hardly a boat on the river didn't have at least one aerosol can of mosquito repellent aboard. Martha got the can her father carried from a little locker and sprayed his arms while he rowed. She also sprayed herself.

As she put the can back she said, "Mister

Richards said New York City's no place for new-lyweds, Andy."

"He's right. But what else is there?"

She didn't answer. They'd discussed his chances of securing employment in Carleton the night before.

He made a face. "Yeah I know — lobster fishing."

She coloured a little at the way he'd said that. Not that she had any illusions concerning her father, but because he was, after all, still her father. He saw that in the failing twilight and looked swiftly contrite.

"I didn't mean it like it sounded, Marty. I meant . . . we don't want to live like that — do we?"

She shook her head in agreement but she also said, "We're just not going to be able to start at the top, Andy."

They were abreast of the rotting, tilting old boat-landing where the decaying old *Carleton Hotel* stood in its mournful setting of underbrush and gaunt old trees. Since childhood, both had known of this spot as "haunted."

The *Carleton Hotel* was what remained of the turn-of-the-century "spa" which had brought be-whiskered men and ostrich-plumed ladies up from New York City. It had long since reverted to the county on the delinquent tax lists and although every three years it was advertised for sale on the tax rolls, everyone was resigned to it sitting out there with the underbrush slowly choking it, until it either fell down or lightning struck it.

Every window had been broken, all the plumbing fixtures had long since been wrenched out. Most of the doors were also gone, but at one time it had been a quite handsome two-storied mansion-type hostelry with great white columns and a broad wooden porch. To prevent children from being lost out there, or possibly hurt, people had been saying the old hotel was haunted for forty years.

As Andy and Martha looked, a gold-grey owl soared over the roof and beat his way on silent wings out across the river. Andy laughed. "It's a witch," he said, and shipped his oars to let her father's boat drift in towards the shore where a tangle of thorny creepers stood on either side of the gloomy path.

She smiled at his joke but when he tied up and stepped ashore she made no immediate move to follow. He turned offering a hand. Finally, she arose, but said, "Where are you going? There's nothing up there worth seeing." As she stepped on shore and looked up, she gave his fingers a convulsive little squeeze. "Andy; it's getting late. We really ought to start back."

He broke through the creepers making the trail easier for her. Where they emerged upon what had once been a spacious lawn and which now was a small jungle, he said, "It's been years since I've been up here, Marty. Four of us came up to spend the night and see spooks." He smiled as he waited for her to come up. "There were rats in the walls but we didn't stay to make sure. And there was no moon like there is tonight."

She was shallowly breathing. She knew it was ridiculous to fear anything as harmless as an old ruined building but she said, "It's just so — quiet," and reached out to detain him as he turned to move up closer. He took her hand tugging her along.

Shadows softened ravages of time and neglect. Moonlight helped by making the darkness less sooty; it also shone back off the sluggish Pawtucket. They went as far as the porch and there, because her fingers were cold in his hand, he stopped, drew her down beside him on the broad, sagging old steps, and leaned back to gaze down towards the crumbling boat-dock and flowing river.

"Can you imagine what all this was like a half century ago, Marty?" he asked.

She nodded. "Very elegant. With horses and buggies and women with long dresses and men with bushy sideburns and bowler hats."

"There's a series of hot-water pools out back. Did you ever see them?"

"No and I don't want to see them now, either, Andrew Weatherby."

He turned, smiling an impish smile. "You're not afraid of ghosts."

"How do you know I'm not? I've never seen one."

He laughed aloud and she smiled back at him.

"If I can help it I'm never going to see one either." She looked around and back again. "Why did you want to come here; it's depressing."

He shrugged. He hadn't, as a matter of fact, thought ahead to this place at all. It had just happened to be where he was beginning to tire from rowing. "It's a beautiful setting. The best one along the river in fact. Imagine what it'd look like with the underbrush burnt off, the lawn planted again, the old hotel fixed up, the road resurfaced."

"For what?" she demanded. "Who'd come here when they could stay at modern hotels in town?"

He turned, studied her a moment, then reached with both arms. "What makes you so practical all the time?" he asked, then covered her lips with his mouth so she couldn't answer.

Chapter Six

Summertime New England has a clean smell to it. On full-moon nights it's as though there couldn't possibly be a place called Up-state New York or a city with millions in it anywhere in the world, let alone within commuting distance of the countryside.

The way Andy put it was best. "There are two worlds. Ours and — *theirs.*"

She thought he'd been thinking of his father — his father's world — when he'd said that. She had no answer because she was by nature exactly as he'd said earlier — before the kiss. She was practical.

Once, she'd had illusions. Once she'd even been convinced a lover would come — not clad in armour or mounted upon a white steed — but in a powerful, sleek boat on the Pawtucket. Two years at *Carleton High School* had withered every dream; even the capacity to dream. She was Mike O'Toole's girl from shantytown.

"I've got to find a way," muttered Andy, leaning back upon the rotting steps, head in his hands, his thick chest pushed out and arched while he gazed up at the purple sky. "Marty; there's got to be a way."

"There is," she said, turning, lifting a hard, brown hand and placing it upon his chest while she watched the square shadow under his jaw. "But as I said, Andy, this is just the first day."

He grunted. "There'll be fifty more just like it, too. Unless I can come up with something."

"Such as?"

He rolled his eyes, looking at her. "I don't know. Something. There are too many people in New York, Marty. They're all either looking for new jobs or trying to find better ones. I can keep going down there until I wear out my shoes, and if I'm lucky I'll land something that'll get us moved and settled. And there we'll vegetate."

She ran her hand higher, through his crinkly hair and down the side of his smooth cheek. "At least we'll vegetate together, Andy."

He jerked free and sat up shaking his head. "I've heard my father say it a dozen times. The only way anyone gets ahead in this life is by using brain, not brawn. I've got to figure that out."

She let her hand drop away, turned and considered the river again. Finally, she leaned back, elbows upon the step above and behind her. She was a sturdy girl, round and solid as stone. Her breast thrust upwards. He turned to speak, hung silent for a moment gazing at her, then reached, twisting her to him with powerful arms. She didn't resist. She loved him very much. She scarcely thought of anything else when he wasn't around, and when he *was* around she *couldn't* think of anything else.

But his kiss made a warning burn up through her. She clung, feeling his muscles, his vital nearness, and relished the wickedness that told her to kiss back the same way. But she didn't, she felt the full heat of his hunger and waited until he loosened a little, then got free and jumped up, cheeks aflame but not visibly so in the warm gloom of full night.

"We've got to get back," she said, and turned looking down at him. "Andy . . . ?"

He slowly stood up, reluctantly it seemed. "Yes?"

"Go see Mister Richards."

He'd evidently forgotten because he owlishly blinked. She took his hand and tugged him along back down the slope where the boat bobbed on a lazy current. He said nothing until, pushing off again, turning the little craft so it would drift stern-first with the tide, he used only one oar, holding it in close like a paddle and making it serve as their tiller.

"That's another thing," he said. "It was my fault John got fired. I knew my father wouldn't like it that he didn't stop me the other night."

"How could he have stopped you? You were upset, that night."

"Nevertheless it was my fault old John got fired."

She showed a little exasperation. "Andy; Mister Richards is a grown man. He can look out for himself. We've got other things to think about, haven't we?"

His eyes moved slowly to her face, his expression different. In an almost lazy tone he said, "Is that what men mean when they say women nag?"

She blushed. "I suppose it is. I'm sorry."

He smiled. For a moment it seemed he might try moving up into the bow towards her but he didn't, which was just as well; the boat wasn't that foolproof.

They came to the creek and turned in. There was a light on at the house which meant her father was home. Neither of them mentioned that, nor that it was about nine o'clock either, which wasn't late enough to cause anyone to worry anyway.

They tethered the boat and she slow-paced along beside him around the house to his car. Her father's homemade truck was out there too, parked ten feet from the convertible. They caught the aroma of food cooking. She said it was her father.

"Sometimes when he comes home he's as hungry as a bear."

Andrew opened his arms. She went up against him her full length. They kissed then she buried her face upon his chest. "I don't want to wait, Andy. I've never wanted to."

"Nor I," he whispered, nuzzling her crisp dark hair. "Especially on a night like. . . . Marty?"

"No," she whispered, breaking clear. "Where'll you stay tonight after you see Mister Richards?"

He shrugged. It wasn't important. Anyway that's not what he was thinking; he knew why she'd asked it too. So they'd start thinking along a new course.

"Maybe I'll get a room."

She nodded, put her hands upon his chest and studied the shirt buttons as though she'd never seen shirt buttons before. She didn't seem twenty years old right then, small and girlish as she was.

He said, "The moonlight sure makes you pretty."

She wrinkled her nose at him. "But not so good in broad daylight, huh Andy?"

He reached swiftly but she was even quicker. From six feet off she said, "Where will you look tomorrow? New York again?"

He dropped his arms, turned and climbed into the car. "I don't know. Not New York. Today was enough. Maybe I'll go somewhere and try to figure out what I ought to do." He leaned out the door. "Are you going to kiss me good night?"

She shook her head keeping the distance between them. "We'll wear it out. Good luck tomorrow, Andy — remember: I love you."

She turned and fled around the far side of the house. He sat for ten seconds after she'd disappeared before starting the car, backing around and shooting back up towards the lighted part of town past the sentinel poplars and the flowering rose bushes.

The night was pleasant with patches of fragrance, enough humidity near the river to keep it from being objectionably warm, and in town the moonlight made street lamps superfluous. When Andrew parked out front of the hotel he glanced up along the second-storey windows. He had known John Richards as one who retired early and who arose the same way. A few lights were glowing up there. About as many windows were dark. Since he didn't know yet which window was John's he got out of the car and started towards the porch to find out. He never reached the lobby.

From warm shadow a distinguishable soft drawl said, "Thought I'd be abed, didn't you, boy?"

Andy swung, but the north reaches of the porch were in full shadow. He walked towards the voice. Old John had his feet cocked up on the railings, his wide shoulders set against the tilted-back chair. He motioned towards another chair.

"To be right truthful," he spoke on, still in that mild drawl, "I slept two hours this afternoon." He chuckled. "Never had much use for folks that'd sleep in the workin' hours of the day, Andy. Used to figure they was either lazy or old." John paused to look over. "Now I've never been lazy so that means I finally got there, don't it?"

Andy didn't know what to say, exactly, so he simply sat and looked up and down the roadway, which was quiet except for a few people leaving the motion picture house a square away.

"No luck in the city, huh?" muttered old John.

"Not a bit."

"I'd have been suspicious if you'd had any."

"Why?"

"Whoever won on the first roll o' the dice?" John shifted positions. "Time changes, Andy. When I was your age a feller sallied forth and made himself a place. Nowadays, seems to me there's just gettin' to be too many folks. Nowadays a man's got to grab the first thing that comes along — like it or not — else he's got to wait until he's broke and hungry, then take the *last* thing that comes along — which won't be anything he'd like, either, just like the first time."

"Suppose nothing comes along, John?"

"Well; something'll come along. How soon it comes along depends on you."

"I got two blisters from walking today."

"Yeah but you're sittin' here tonight, aren't you?"

Andrew turned. John was calmly gazing at him with the moonlight working around to where it could filter through into their dark corner. It had already diluted the darkness enough to smooth away most of the sun-squint and age-etchings making John look about as he might have appeared thirty, forty years back — long, lean wide-shouldered, slow-talking and shrewd.

"You mean you think I ought to be out hunting a job *now?*"

"Son; wouldn't be anyone else out doin' that tonight. And no fooling about it, you *need* one, don't you? Sure; right now you're down in the dumps. It's like getting bucked off in the middle of a cussed desert and not knowin' which way to commence walking. But one thing's danged sure, Andy, you're going to have to walk *somewhere*. In your case mopin' around in the dark or settin' with Martha don't help one damned bit. What you need is a job; that's what you got to concentrate on every wakin' moment."

A couple walked past out on the sidewalk hand-in-hand. For as long as their swaying figures were visible Andrew said nothing. Even afterwards he sat for a long moment, looking out towards the roadway.

"Maybe it's a mite late now," went on John Richards. "Folks'll be abed. But dawn comes early and it stays light this time o' year until nine at night."

Andrew sank back in his chair, rummaged a pocket, brought forth a packet of chewing gum and offered a stick of it to John, who shook his head.

"Chewed too much tobacco in my time to get much of a kick out o' that stuff, son."

"I thought of something tonight," he told the older man, popping a stick of gum into his mouth. "I rowed Marty up by the old hotel this evening. It's a regular forest up there."

"Sure is. I walked up there once, a year or so back."

"Summer'll be gone in another couple of months, John."

The older man was watching his guest now with steady eyes. "Sure will. Commence getting cold then too."

"That's right, John."

"What did you think about, son?"

"Suppose, instead of hunting high and low and coming up with some job that'll barely feed me, I struck out on my own. At least I'd be utilising the time I'd otherwise be wasting looking for a job."

"How?"

"Get a permit from the county to clean up around the old *Carleton Hotel.*"

They looked at one another. Old John, with no inkling how anyone could profit from doing what Andrew had just mentioned, sat and waited saying nothing.

"It's common knowledge, John, the county'd like to get that piece of land back onto the tax rolls. It'll never happen when you need a guide just to work your way through the forest to reach the place."

"So you figure to get the county to hire you to clear off the land. Is that it?"

"Partly, John. The other part is — with a good chain saw I could rack up the trees I cut down and sell firewood."

Old John thought a moment then slowly smiled. "You see," he said, sounding pleased. "That's what I meant. Keep concentratin' on your problem and the answer'll come. Use night-time just like you'd use day-time." He slapped his knee. "All right; when'll you go see if you can work it out?"

"First thing in the morning. But . . ."

"Yeah? You need money for the chain saw?"

Andrew shook his head. "I've got enough money in my checking account. But — it'll mean Marty and I can't get married for at least another two months."

"Pshaw, boy; that's nothing to stew over. You already been a year without, and durin' that time you couldn't even *see* your way clear. This way, at least you got some idea how long it'll be. Two months goes by awful fast when you're working hard. Believe me on that."

Chapter Seven

There was an incongruity of which Andrew was aware the moment he entered the County Court House the following day in the fact that the son of perhaps the wealthiest man in the county was trying to locate someone who could tell him who to see about getting a job as clean-up-man around the tumble-down old *Carleton Hotel.* The girl at the reception desk who doubled as switch-board operator, sent Andrew to the Director of Public Works, then at once called several friends to tell them this surprising piece of gossip.

The Director of Public Works heard Andrew out then said he'd have to first see the Tax Collector, then get approval from the Chairman of the Board of Supervisors, *then* come back and see the Director of Public Works.

The way the Director explained it, the whole routine seemed perfectly rational to him even though to Andy it sounded both redundant and stifling. Nevertheless, he saw, first, the Tax Collector, then the Chairman of Supervisors.

The Tax Collector was also the assessor and County Appraiser. He was a hirsute individual with thick glasses and a wide chest which had slipped badly and rested now just behind a straining belt. He was courteous and attentive, but he also seemed to scent more to Andrew's idea than he was told. Finally, when he said it sounded like a worthwhile idea, and since it wouldn't cost the County any more, he'd approve, but — and here he peered sceptically from behind his glasses at Andrew — if all this was some scheme hatched by — well — perhaps someone else with the money to develop the old hotel, the County would re-assess it as soon as the work was finished.

Andrew sorted that out as he climbed stairs in search of the Chairman of the Board of County Supervisors. It didn't dawn on him that the Tax Collector had suspected perhaps Andy's father was somehow behind the scheme, until he found the Chairman.

This was the crucial interview and Andy's heart sank. The Chairman was an egotistical balding man who combed what hair he retained in a strategic fashion to cover as much scalp as possible. He was also gimlet-eyed, smoked foul cigars and projected his personality as though he were some kind of tycoon instead of a small-town part-time official who ran a trinket business on the side.

He listened, asked a few questions, then got on the telephone to call someone named "George," whom he kept patronisingly calling by that name throughout the conversation. He wanted to know what legalities might be involved. "George" evidently told him as long as no lease was signed, only a permit to cut the timber and make the improvements at no expense to the County, there was nothing to be apprehensive about.

The Chairman then beamed his insincere, superior smile and sent Andrew back to the Director of Public Works. Meanwhile, he telephoned that individual repeating what "George" had told him so that by the time Andrew walked into the Director's office, the paunchy individual was beaming.

"Go right ahead," he told Andrew. "We'll have a permit issued." The Director leaned upon his desk studying Andrew. "I'd like to ask one personal question," he said, smiling. "Aren't you going back to college this fall?"

Andrew was not going back and said so. The Director absorbed this with a gentle nod. He had a son, he said, who knew of Andrew at school. The Director thought it was too bad, after going this far, Andrew would drop out now.

The curiosity which followed him throughout the Court House was almost strong enough to lean against. He had the feeling of people reaching for telephones the moment he left their offices. He didn't lose that feeling until he got back outside in the clean fresh air. He also came away from the Court House with a stirring comprehension of what his father and others had meant when they'd referred to bureaucrats and civil leaches.

By the time he got back to see John Richards it was two o'clock. By the time he got down to see Martha it was four and her father insisted Andrew stay for supper, an invitation he accepted although he'd meant to get over to Hanson's hardware store and buy the chain saw so he'd be ready to start work the following morning. In fact, two hours later when he and Martha were walking along the creek-bank, he felt guilty about having put that off. He could feel old John's disapproval.

Martha was pleased that Andrew had worked out something but she was also doubtful about the merit of the idea. She said, "Suppose you can't sell the wood, Andy?"

Of course he could sell the wood; anyone who'd ever looked out over the rooftops of Carleton any winter day knew there was woodsmoke rising from just about every chimney.

"But people heat with gas and electricity and oil," she said. "They don't really *heat* with wood any more. At Christmastime maybe, and New Year's Eve, but — "

"Marty if they only burned wood those times and everyone bought from us, that'd do it. That'd sell us out."

But she still worried. "Did you ever run a chain saw before?"

He hadn't, but as he said, he'd never driven a

car before he tried it. He'd never learned to swim until he'd been in the water. He got a little exasperated with her. "Marty; what a man needs from his friends is encouragement, not doubt all the time."

"I'm sorry, Andy. It just seems — well — not what I thought would work out for us."

"We have to start somewhere, don't we?"

"And you'll be quitting college just at the time when you'd be ready for your final semester. Oh Andy I feel terrible because it's my fault. You'd have been so much better off if you'd never seen me."

He smiled, stopped and took her into his arms. She was small when compared to him but that made her fit into his embrace all the better. She didn't lift her face so he put a finger under her chin and lifted. "As old John would say, dear, anyone would be better off if they never met someone else — but they *do* meet folks." He kissed her. She placed both hands flat against his chest savouring the softness of his mouth, the warmth and gentleness, then raised both arms, locked them around his neck and suddenly gave his head a rough pull forward. She let him feel the hunger then for a moment, but the moment his biceps hardened she turned aside her face and, still holding him, said, "How will you find customers for the wood?"

It was so irrelevant he hung there for a moment, then threw back his head and laughed. She got free and ruefully smiled.

"Someday I won't be able to think of things," she told him. "That'll be the day we're both in trouble."

He kept smiling as they resumed their way. They passed her father's old boat, passed some rotting stumps where someone else had once had a landing, wound in and out of the underbrush and tall trees until the creek began to narrow, then he stopped to look at the moon in a delightful little fen where punky stumps showed that many decades ago a man had cut wood here.

It was close to nine o'clock. Mike didn't care how late his daughter stayed as long as she was with Andrew Weatherby. He'd made that amply clear when they'd first started going together. Nevertheless Martha had never willingly stayed out past ten, so while Andrew was gazing at the star-washed sky she sat gingerly on a rotting stump and said, "You could sleep at our place tonight, Andy. I'd get you up early enough to go down to Hanson's, buy the saw and go up there to start work."

He dropped his eyes to her lifted, golden-tan face. It was a round girlish face with strength showing. The lips were wide, the lower one with a heaviness at the centre. The eyes, like midnight, watched him with dark softness. The nose was tipped a little, still with a few of girlhood's tiny freckles across it.

"What in the devil," he said slowly and just a trifle thickly, "could my father see in you to object to?"

70

She didn't alter expression at all. "For one thing I'm Mike O'Toole's daughter. For another I'm from down here by the creek. Then of course there'd be the things that *really* matter."

"Like?"

"Well; you mentioned them once. The social amenities — which fork to use, which colour to wear."

He nodded slightly without speaking but still keeping his eyes steadily upon her. She'd ticked off the objections one by one.

"If you were married to a common woodcutter — what then?"

She smiled. "Why then I guess folks would say I dragged you down to my level. Andy; you'd better face it now — as long as we live it'll always be you who married beneath you. It'll always be me who'll cause you humiliation and embarrassment. Not because I want to — I'll learn about the forks and the proper colours, but Carleton will never forget."

"Carleton can go to hell," he said.

She shrugged, half agreeing, half disagreeing. "*We* may may feel that way, but we're still going to live here, aren't we?"

"Sure." He made a savage gesture with one brawny arm. "I'll clear the land all the way up to the Smokerise Mountains just so's we *can* live here." He let the arm drop. "No; not really. After we're married and I've finished with the wood we'll find something else — something better." He sank down upon the old stump beside her. It groaned ominously under their combined weight. "The secret is — do it yourself. Old John confirmed that last night, but I was beginning to think of it myself after that forlorn day in the city. Do it yourself. Be an employer not an employee." He covered her hand with his big paw. "We'll make out. We'll be married in September."

She looked at him with her lips softening, her dark eyes gently glowing. It was the first time either of them had ever dared set an actual *time;* they'd known of course that eventually they'd be wed, but up until this moonlit night neither had ever been able to honestly set a specific time for it.

She leaned upon his shoulder. "Autumn," she whispered, "when the leaves are turning."

He said, "When folks'll be starting to burn wood," and gave a little laugh as she raised her head.

"Now who's being practical, Andy?"

They arose and started back. An owl moaned at their passing and down by the river some startled animal sprang into the water when their huge shadows passed by. The moon was smoky this night, the air as still and warm as dawn.

He broke trail through the rankest part for her and when they emerged back by the stumps where a boat-landing had once stood she stopped to pluck a piece of wood from her hair. He watched. For a little girl she was big in some ways, and as strong as a man; a lot of girls her age wiggled when they walked. She didn't. There wasn't a ripple anywhere. A lot of girls laughed more than she did, but when she *did* laugh — or just when she smiled — the whole world became a brighter place.

He took her hand and started forward again. They reached the boat and her father was standing there smoking. He'd heard them coming and turned to show his face in the moonlight. He was wearing a little sly smile but all he said was: "Fine night. Warm as daytime."

They stopped. Martha looked closely at her father. In good light she'd have been able to tell in a minute whether or not he'd been drinking. It was more difficult like this. If he'd been drinking he'd be talkative — he'd also have innuendoes to offer which was what she feared.

"Saw Mist' Richards up town a while back," said Mike, taking a pull off his cigarette then flipping it out towards the centre of the creek. "Him and Miz' Moody." Mike's smile settled a little tugging the edges of his mouth slightly downward. "They make quite a pair — him tall and gaunt, her short and thick."

Andrew kept watching Mike O'Toole. He didn't exactly *dis*like him. On the other hand he wasn't fond of him either. He'd made a point of avoiding him as much as he could, but because that wasn't always possible he had a kind of wary attitude when around the older man. Now suspecting Mike would say more about old John and Rachel, he spoke up.

"They're friends, Mister O'Toole."

"Sure," agreed Martha's father, and leered. "At their ages what else can they be?"

Martha reddened, took resolute hold of Andrew's hand and started past up towards the house. Her father turned, plunged both hands into his trouser pockets and seemed about to speak. As Andrew shouldered past, though, Mike changed his mind, shrugged and turned back to considering his boat and the river. Andy had caught a whiff of his breath. He'd been drinking all right.

Up behind the house where they halted beside Andrew's car Martha said, with a low sigh of relief, "Sometimes he just — says things. Anyway I think he's been drinking."

Andrew nodded and pushed Mike out of their talk.

"I'll be back tomorrow night to let you know how it went, the first day as a woodcutter." He grinned. "My father'd have a fit. . . ."

"Andy? Would you consider going home tonight and — talking to him?"

"What about? I'm not giving you up and that's all there is to it, Marty. That's what he'd want as the price of patching things up."

"Well; but you could try, couldn't you?"

Andrew shook his head. "No, I'm not going to try. He had his say, I had mine. I'm not going back. If there's any more talk he'll have to start it. That's about as likely as that moon up there falling down."

She raised her face to see the moon and he

stepped up, took her by the hips and swayed her to him bringing his head down fast. She gasped. The kiss was sudden and passionate. But he let her go almost at once.

She blinked and straightened her dress. "I wasn't expecting that one," she said, and smiled. "But you'll notice I didn't exactly fight."

He stepped round her to the car. "It wouldn't have done you any good if you had. See you tomorrow night."

She nodded and stood in the moonlight watching him start the car, back clear, swing about and drive off. The old moon was more smoky-looking than ever. She turned and heavily walked back towards the house.

Chapter Eight

There was nothing complicated, Andrew discovered, about operating a chain saw, but there were several tricks that made it easier, and the whine was something he'd just have to get used to. One trick, he discovered before noon that first day, was to keep several little rat-tail files for filing the teeth of the chain. They had to be filed often and at a particular angle or they chewed their way through the wood instead of cutting through.

By two in the afternoon he made another discovery; when the saw was cutting properly it spat out a feathery trail of fine shavings. When the chain-teeth were dull the shavings came out more like sawdust, and when that happened he had to use more weight to make the saw bite into wood.

There was also the matter of remembering to punch the oiler plunger to keep the chain moving smoothly around the saw-bar.

But the technicalities weren't hard to master.

By four o'clock when he'd cut down and bucked up two fair-sized oaks, he thought he understood the rudiments of operating his saw. The fact that it was new and therefore functioned perfectly helped him learn under ideal conditions.

What surprised him, though, was the amount of wood one man could put down and buck up into fireplace lengths in one day. When he stopped to eat a tin of devilled ham and drink a half gallon of milk he'd brought along for his lunch, he made some mental calculations. Granting he was a little optimistic, and also granting the price of cordwood was what he thought it was, he'd already earned twenty dollars.

He was dirty and scratched and sore in every muscle, but happy. Even the reflection that he wouldn't actually collect that twenty dollars for another month or two didn't dampen his ardour. He *would* get it and that was what mattered.

He'd earned the first money in his life he'd ever made entirely through his own resources. It was a thrilling sensation. He didn't even mind the mosquitoes, the heat, the torn trousers or the aches that increased as the day wore along until five o'clock when he could have quit but didn't. He sawed wood until nearly seven and only quit then because he'd promised to see Martha.

He'd bought a bedroll from the same hardware store where he'd bought the chain saw, the files, and cans for chain saw fuel. The old hotel solved his problem of where to stay very nicely. Not at all elegantly; not even conveniently because he had to wait until sunset to wade out into the Pawtucket for his bath, but it was free board and that had strong appeal.

By the time he'd cleaned up it was nearly dark. By the time he got down to the creek it wasn't just dark, it was *pitch* dark. That old full moon wouldn't be up until one hour later. It would keep coming up later as it diminished in size until it failed to show at all, then eventually re-emerged thin as a curved dagger, ready to start through its entire mystical cycle again.

Mike had taken a big catch of lobster up to town earlier and hadn't returned, but as Martha told him outside on the cool, dark porch, since this was Saturday night she wouldn't expect to see him before morning anyway.

They talked of his work. She got salve for the scratches and made little commiserating sounds over his sore muscles. She said she'd meant to row up and visit but her father hadn't come back with the boat until almost two in the afternoon which wouldn't have given her adequate time. She also said she'd met John Richards up in town and he'd told her not to worry, that things had a way of working themselves out when folks really worked at it.

She also asked if he'd be going round to see old John. He would, he told her, but not until the following evening because he was too tired tonight.

She brought him a glass of cold juice from inside and said her father had mentioned hearing the saw when he'd been upriver a ways. He sipped the juice, said it didn't seem as though he'd ever get enough liquid, and left after an hour and a half because he was drowsy.

She went back inside, was working in the kitchen and didn't hear a car, or any other sound for that matter, until someone's heavy knuckles grated across the door out front. She knew who it *wasn't* — her father or Andrew — so her heart missed a beat. She made no immediate move to go answer the knocking either. When it was eventually repeated she relented enough to step forth and call out asking who was there. The answer told only half the story.

"Richards, Martha. John Richards."

She opened up with relief flooding through her. Old John stood out there his head dropped a little so he'd be able to clear the upper jamb, and very erect and prim at his side was Rachel Moody. Martha knew Rachel by sight and nodded. John drawled out an introduction then waited to be invited inside. Martha obliged, uneasy under the tart, hard look John's companion shot left and right round the room as she entered.

John looked slightly dubious, as though whatever his mission he wasn't exactly delighted at being about it. Martha asked them to be seated. She waited until Rachel sat then asked if they'd like coffee. They wouldn't, Rachel said. She then made a forthright long study of Martha, held her purse in her lap and sat very stiffly.

It was John who made it easier all round. He grinned and said, "Seen that wood-cuttin' man this evening, Missy?"

Martha nodded quickly, glad the ice had been broken. "He left not more than fifteen minutes ago."

"Been at it has he?"

She smiled at old John. "He's sore and scratched and tired tonight. He tore his trousers but he thinks he made twenty dollars today."

John turned as though to challenge Rachel to say something. She didn't; she was still evidently coming to some kind of conclusion about Martha. She said, "I had an idea you'd be — different — Miss O'Toole."

Martha's eyes widened. "Different, Mrs. Moody?"

"*Miss* Moody."

"I'm sorry."

"Nothing to be sorry about. Person my age should be married. I thought you'd be — well — bigger."

John smiled and dropped a wink at Martha. "Rachel; best things come in small packages."

Rachel's Yankee-blue eyes shone with just a hint of a smile. "John, she's pretty as a picture."

"Well I told you didn't I?"

"Pshaw; you tell me lots of things. Miss O'Toole — Martha isn't it?"

"Yes."

"Do you mind . . . ?"

Martha smiled. "I wish you would, Miss Moody."

"Fine. Now then, Martha, we came along to tell you Andrew's father was looking for him in town today."

"Oh? Maybe they'll — resolve things."

"Humph," snorted Rachel. "Not likely. But John and I talked a bit, and we've a notion Mister Weatherby's going to hear about the wood-cutting enterprise. We think he'll try to stop it and send Andrew back to college."

Martha nodded slightly; she hadn't considered this at all but she could see that it made sound sense. Old John crossed one long leg over the other one, slouched in his chair and, still looking pleasantly cheerful, said, "Missy; it's not right a man and his son shouldn't love'n respect one another. What I'm trying to say is — maybe if Andy went back to college this last semester, then cut wood afterwards, it'd help smooth things out." He didn't give Martha a chance to speak whether she might have done so or not. "Now it's not that I'm not one-hundred per cent behind him, you hear. I am. Otherwise I wouldn't have egged him on like I did. But Rachel's right about how a man and his son ought to feel towards one another."

Rachel interrupted. "I think by now Mister Weatherby has seen the error of his ways. At least it seems to me — and I've known the whole family since Andy was just a baby — those two ought to meet again. Just the two of them, mind you, which is the real reason John and I came along here tonight."

Martha was in the dark. "You want me to help, is that it?"

John nodded. "He'd never go back home, would he?"

Martha shook her head. "I asked him to last night. He refused."

"Fine," said old John. "Then suppose when he comes here tomorrow night . . . he will come won't he?"

"Yes, he'll be here," replied Martha, beginning to understand.

"Well fine," John exclaimed. "And Rachel and I'll fetch his pappy down too. Then maybe the three of us could just sort of fade out into the brush for a spell. What do you think, Missy?"

Martha knew exactly what she thought. "Mister Richards; Andy'll think I've done that to him. He'll think I — "

"No," interposed Rachel. "We'll see to it the entire meeting is accidental."

Martha was sceptical. "Mister Weatherby is no fool, I'm sure, and I *know* Andy isn't."

Rachel sat a moment in sober thought. Old John who had seemed to defer to her, did so now. He sat and studied the worn toe of one shoe and said nothing. Martha arose, went to the stove, put on the coffee pot and returned to her chair. That gave her a moment to gather her thoughts.

She said, "Miss Moody; suppose I got Andy to

take me for a drive up to that little café north of town tomorrow night? Wouldn't it seem more believable — that way?"

Rachel looked at John. He shrugged, still deferring. She looked back at Martha and nodded. "I don't know just how we'll get Mister Weatherby to that place, but we'll manage it, won't we John?"

"Yes'm."

"We'll have to." Rachel arose and smiled for the first time. "You keep a clean house, Martha. And, as John said, you're very pretty. But I still for some reason thought you'd be a larger girl."

John arose, looked wistfully towards the aromatic coffee pot and turned to hold the door for Rachel. He winked again at Martha.

"Nothing wrong at all in what you're doing," he said. "Ten years from now when you tell Andy he'll agree with me. Only I wouldn't tell him much sooner."

She walked out into the darkness with them, looked for the car which wasn't there and understood finally why they'd caught her by surprise: They'd walked from town. Rachel stopped to consider a struggling bed of tangled geraniums. "Soapy water'll perk them up," she said. "Martha. . . ."

"Yes?"

Rachel looked at the girl balancing additional words on her tongue but in the end didn't utter them. They'd have been soft words, evidently. Soft words didn't come easily to New Englanders.

"Don't feel like you're betraying Andrew," Rachel said, finally controlling her emotions and speaking briskly again. "You're a girl that'd want for him what John and I want — the best that's good for him."

Rachel reached with a spear-like motion, took hold of Martha's hand, squeezed, dropped the hand and swiftly moved off.

Old John winked back for the last time and strode away beside Miss Moody, his long, easy stride covering as much ground with half the effort. They were lost in the darkness within minutes. Martha could still hear their footfalls over the gravel long after she could no longer see them.

She went back as far as the sagging front porch. There, she sat down where she could see fireflies and hear the creek. She argued with herself. She had agreed to do as Rachel wanted without even a struggle, but now, with reaction setting in, she wasn't at all sure she'd acted properly.

It wasn't that she didn't approve of Andy and his father patching up their differences. She did want that. But she was fearful that if Andy found out what she'd agreed to do without telling him, he'd be terribly disappointed in her.

She wasn't even sure she wouldn't be just as disappointed in herself.

Then she heard her father's auto coming and because she didn't want to face him right at this

moment she jumped up and fled into her bedroom, closed the door and undressed in darkness, slid into bed — and couldn't go to sleep for
hours.

Chapter Nine

The following morning Martha took the boat out. Not to set traps, neither she nor her father worked on Sunday, but to row upriver and visit with Andrew.

She'd spent an hour making a picnic lunch which rested now in the bow of the boat in its wicker basket. Her father had still been sleeping when she'd left, so she'd made his breakfast then put it in the oven to stay warm.

Earlier, when the bells had rung up in town, she stopped as she usually did to listen to them. She hadn't gone to church in over a year. Her father had said it wasn't necessary and she'd agreed with him. But she'd never been able to believe that — not altogether anyway — because she'd been to church many times in her lifetime so she knew, without having any idea *why*, that going to church was good for people. They felt better for it.

But one didn't appear in church in a four or five year old dress. Not in Carleton, one didn't.

She rowed with the morning warmth giving the river a steely sheen. When she was abreast of a low headland her father called "salt spit" she cocked her head. It was about here her father had said he'd heard the saw. She heard nothing. Perhaps Andy wasn't working because it was Sunday. Perhaps the Sabbath didn't mean much elsewhere but it did in rock-bound — and hide-bound — New England.

There was very little tide running this morning and the heat hadn't really built up yet. There were no other boats on the river yet either but before the day was done there'd be some. Most of the "estate-people" as the natives called them, came up from the city on week-ends. Almost without exception they boated.

She saw the rotting landing up ahead and pulled closer to shore. She even tried to peer up the slope to sight the old hotel. There was too much underbrush.

She didn't tie up at the old pylons but tethered her craft nearer the little footpath — and found a not-quite-white towel spread to dry upon some bushes farther back. She smiled. There was a large bar of soap and some shaving things on a plank there too.

Andy had hacked the undergrowth clear for the full distance of the path from river to open slope. She had no trouble walking up there at all, even with the picnic hamper, but as she got closer and the silence came down to meet her, it began to dawn upon her that perhaps he wasn't around. She bit her lip; she should have told him the night before.

Then she heard it. The steady sound of someone heaving green wood. It was a dull, solid sound. She went ahead until she saw the movement. He was racking up cordwood. She stopped, astonished, for back through the clearing where the sun shone through for the first time in many years were at least a dozen of those even, doubled-up ricks, each with poles driven into the ground at both ends. Each with the white, raw butts of cut wood glowing in the sunshine.

She knew nothing about wood; that it was measured in tiers or cords, but she was surprised at the amount of it he'd cut and the size of the clearing he'd made.

He was working shirtless and hatless, an old pair of oil-stained dungarees held about his lean waist with a black belt. She watched him a moment. He was strong. Muscles rippled as he flung the pieces of wood upon their stacks. The sun had bronzed him; it had also made his crinkly hair paler than usual. He worked without waste motion, trouser legs cut off four or six inches above the boot-tops.

She put aside the hamper where there was some shade and called. He turned at once, startled, and for a moment after he'd straightened up, just looked. Then his face curled with a broad grin, he wiped his hands upon the oily trousers and turned to walk over.

"A wood sprite," he said, his eyes laughing down at her. "I was just thinking about you." He saw the wicker basket. "Lobster," he said.

"Chicken. Fried chicken." She held him off. "You're oily."

She was wearing dungarees and a pale blue shirt, her ordinary clothing, but she didn't want the grease on her so she leaned and he leaned. They kissed like that, neither touching the other except with their lips.

"You're beautiful," he said, still silently laughing at her. "Or maybe it's lust because I haven't seen a girl in such a long while."

"Since last night. That's not such a long while."

"It is when all I've seen since were owls, a grass snake or two — and that saw over there."

She strolled up with him to the stacks of wood. "How did you ever get so much of it sawed in only two days?"

"I'll show you after a bit. The saw may look small and fragile but you've never seen anything bite through wood the way it does." He gestured, not without pride. "There is three tier in each of those small stacks. That equals one cord of wood. Those larger ricks are two cord each. You're looking at about a hundred dollars worth of wood." He turned towards her, very proud. "In only two days. That's a small fortune each week, more each month. By September we'll be able to rent a decent house in town, buy some furniture and get married." His eyes misted towards her.

"Unless you'd like to back out."

That time she didn't heed the oily trousers when she leaned into him, ran both arms around his naked back and met his lips as they came down to her mouth.

They left the clearing while he showed her what he was doing. It wasn't simply a matter of cutting wood. He was working through the undergrowth and trees towards the old county road, abandoned decades before when people ceased frequenting the hotel. He explained that this had to be done otherwise there'd been no practical route for getting the wood out, once it was sawed and ready.

They wandered through that southwesterly silence with only a few birds to break the ancient hush. It was wonderfully fragrant and cool. Very little sunshine reached through, the earth underfoot was mouldy, and there were wild roses, not much larger than a thumbnail, which blossomed swiftly and lost their petals almost the same day.

He talked a little as they passed along. He estimated how much wood was in a tree for her, pointed out how one had to use strategy to make each cut otherwise the saw had to work too hard.

She listened, marvelling at his enthusiasm. He was scratched, bruised, his hands were skinned, fingernails broken and layered with ground-in grease, but he seemed heedless of these things. She'd never seen him like this before — not just pleased, even proud of himself, but so disreputable-looking. When he halted near a marshy place and pointed out a cluttered spring, she said she thought they ought to go back before the ants found the hamper. He was willing, and took her hand as they walked. His touch was rough. She raised the hand palm up. There were callouses forming.

He laughed.

Back near the hotel he stopped again to consider the stacks of wood. "If I sell it here, fine. If I have to haul it to town. . . ." He looked over where his sleek convertible stood in the centre of a little clearing he'd cut for it. "I'll have to trade the car for a light truck."

She involuntarily said, "Oh, no, Andy." She'd always been so proud of his car.

He looked down, took her hand and led her over beyond the clearing where the hamper stood in deep shade. He said no more on the subject of his car, but she knew, because she knew him, that when the time came he'd trade the convertible for a truck. He was just as fond of the car as she was, but he was turning a little ruthless too, now that he had something other than himself to think about.

She'd brought lemonade, potato salad and fried chicken. He ate with restraint but she saw at once she should have brought twice as much; he ate like a horse.

A motorboat came upriver with a girl and a man in it. They were trowling. They didn't even look towards the old hotel. Later, when Andy was lying back in the leaves, his head propped on

91

one brawny arm, two youths in a trim sailing craft came tacking back and forth against the sluggish tide. From where Martha sat, legs drawn up, arms curled around her knees, she could faintly hear the lilting laughter of the sailors.

Andy said, "Fifteen or sixteen," watching the little craft heel to the helm and dip its sail. "Those are very good years."

She was amused. "You sound like Methuselah."

He grinned. "Sometimes I feel like him. Especially at night when every joint aches."

"Andy . . . ? Come down tonight. We can go for a drive."

He didn't hesitate. "Sure. I'll take you out for dinner." His eyes shone with that sudden spontaneous smile of his. "Last of the big spenders."

She felt a twinge. It had been too easy. She dropped her eyes, then swung to look for the little sailboat. It was gone upriver somewhere. The Pawtucket was as steely quiet and empty as it often was. Her conscience scraped along nerve-ends with steel fingernails. She turned back to speak but he beat her to it.

"We don't really have to wait until September," he said, and that announcement scattered her other thoughts. "There is the wood. I know what I can produce now. We could get married right now, live off the money I have in my school account, and that should carry us over until I sell out up here."

He'd obviously thought this out in advance. She stirred where she sat, mightily tempted, but she shook her head as she said, "September is actually only about six weeks, Andy. Wouldn't it be better to keep the other money — in case you decide to return to school, or if you don't want to do that, so that we'd have something to back us up if anything happened?"

He didn't argue with her logic, which was faultless, but he didn't like the idea either, so he said, "Sometimes you almost make me think you're trying to stall, Marty."

Her eyes flashed and colour crept into each cheek. "Andy; you know that's not true. I'd marry you tomorrow — today in fact — if it wouldn't cause more problems than it would ever solve."

He flung himself backwards upon the leaves looking up through leafy limbs where the glass-clear sky seemed motionless. "The hardest part is the waiting, Marty. Six weeks seems like sixty years." He rolled his head to look as she moved over beside him, and ruefully smiled. "But at least it's something that'll end, isn't it; otherwise, we could only hope. All right; I'll wait."

She put a hand lightly upon his chest, leaned down to lightly kiss him and say, "*We'll* wait."

Two little cockleshells came upriver in what appeared to be a race. The youths in them shouted good-naturedly back and forth as they worked their sails to achieve victory, but because both craft were identical and the crewmen were

93

evenly matched, neither one ever got more than perhaps a fifty foot lead before the other craft came up.

The shouting and straining diverted Andy and Martha. They caught some of the contagious spirit and made a small bet — a kiss. He pulled her down to him when the craft ran past and were lost to sight, neck-and-neck. She didn't resist although she hadn't actually lost the bet.

He smelled good; smelled of wood-sap and wild roses — and oil. The composite was definitely masculine. When her hands encountered his firm flesh it was warm and hard. She rubbed her face against his cheek. He lay there torpidly relaxed from all he'd eaten, from the building heat, from the sense of satisfaction over all he'd accomplished and because as far as he knew there was no real dark cloud on his personal horizon.

He thickly said, "What kind of a wedding? We'll invite John of course — who else?"

She thought of his father but discreetly left this decision to him and said, "Rachel Moody."

For a moment his eyes remained closed then they very slowly opened and turned fully towards her. "Where did you meet Rachel?"

She saw the look, knew she'd inadvertently blundered, and with great relief let it all come out. He sat up, finally, brushed off leaves and looked at her without smiling. "Tonight?" he asked. "They'll have my father out there at the little café — tonight?"

"Yes."

"You'd have helped them against me, Marty?"

She twined her fingers in her lap seeking an honest reply. "I told you, didn't I?" she eventually said defensively, and forced her eyes to his face again.

He plucked a blade of grass, minutely examined it, flung it away and looked straight at her again. "All right, love. We'll just drive out there and have dinner."

She was stopped cold. "You *want* to do that, Andy?"

His voice was low-pitched. "Not especially. But I suppose it won't hurt. Let him find out I don't need him." Andrew's lips lifted in a humourless smile. "Let him see he's not the only Weatherby who can start out with nothing but a strong back." He sprang up, pulled her up and held her at arm's-length. "You dress up tonight, Marty. We'll show him who *we* are!"

Chapter Ten

When she got back home her father had slung an old canvas hammock on the porch and was sleeping in it. He heard her though and raised up the moment a board creaked under her weight. He looked drawn and haggard but at least he'd shaved and had clean dungarees on. He saw the empty hamper and nodded.

"How is the wood cutting progressing?" he asked.

She answered truthfully. "I had no idea anyone could cut so much wood in so short a space of time."

Mike waggled his head. "You'd be surprised. I've seen 'em use those gas-engine-saws upriver a few miles. The noise'd drive me crazy, but then I'd never make a woodsman anyway. But they do a lot of work with those things." He paused, licked his lips and said, "Be a good girl and fetch me a glass of cold water."

She went inside, put the hamper aside and drew the water. Mike was trying to put out the fire in his stomach. He managed to kindle some pretty lively ones on Saturday nights.

Later, with the sun lowering, the sky turning soft red, she made supper for her father, cleaned up around the house to pass the time, and worried.

She had no really stylish clothes. In fact all she'd ever had were house dresses. They'd be all right because it was hot summertime, but none of them were very new. She almost wished she'd talked Andy out of going ahead with it. She could have explained later to Miss Moody and old John.

But she couldn't back out now.

Mike came inside looking no better; his eyes watered and he took the glass to the sink for another drink. But he was pleasant. He usually was, as a matter of fact. He was sly and scheming, but — obviously — he'd never been very successful at that either.

He stood a moment before the picture of Martha's mother in its ornate, tarnished frame atop the china cupboard. The face looking back was dark-eyed and round. Except that the hair was worn longer the picture could almost have been of Martha. Mike turned away, finally, went to the sink and set aside his emptied glass.

"I guess it's set," he said without looking straight at Martha. "You two'll get married. Well; your mother would have approved." He cleared his throat. "Seems funny old Weatherby'd let his boy take off an' turn into wood-cutter though. I thought. . . ."

She knew what he'd thought; Lynne Weatherby, in order to make a better showing for his son, would possibly have moved the O'Tooles up from the shack beside the creek. Mike would want the best for his only child, naturally, but he'd also have his own best interests at heart. He may have been lying out there in the hammock day-dreaming about Mister Weatherby settling a nice lump sum upon him, or maybe allocating Mike so much a month so his daughter-in-law's father wouldn't be just another shantytown dweller.

"He won't always be just a wood-cutter," she said. "And I'm not marrying *Lynne* Weatherby. I'm marrying *Andrew* Weatherby."

"All right, dear, all right. I'm not arguing. Why get sharp with me?"

She didn't answer the query, she simply said, "We're going out for supper tonight. I've got to go bathe and get ready."

As she moved around him he said, "Marty; do you mind telling me your plans?"

She didn't mind. "We're going to be married in September." She watched his face but there was no noticeable change. Of course she hadn't revealed a secret. Everyone had known they would eventually be married.

"September," he mused, and raised his eyes to her. "That's final?"

She nodded and continued on through to her room. Of course it was final. She thought about the finality of it all through the ensuing hour while she got ready. She also reflected upon what a wrenching change it would mean. Not only to her, but to Andy, her father and — she supposed — *his* father.

She did not overlook what his father might try to do at the café tonight — talk Andy into returning to college or at least returning home. But she thought she knew Andrew; knew all of his variety of New Englander. They were a very stubborn people. She'd once had a French-Canadian instructor at *Carleton High School* who had told her there were no more pigheaded people on earth than New Englanders unless it was Old Englanders. He had then waggled a finger and had said, because he could see from her colouring she too was of French-Canadian descent — on her mother's side — there were no more sensible, reasonable, tractable people than French-Canadians so it certainly would appear *le bon Dieu* had known precisely what he'd been up to when he'd put French-Canadians just across the international border from pigheaded New Englanders, so that they could mitigate all the wretched blunders of their neighbours.

It had of course all been facetiously said, but there was a hint of truth in it. She smiled into her mirror. Andrew wouldn't back down for his father or anyone else. She wouldn't want him to. Furthermore, although she'd had doubts about this wood-cutting venture, she had confidence in Andrew and that convinced her he'd pull through.

She brushed her hair until it shone, chose a dress of light cream colour from the meagre selection in her closet, brushed her hair again just before leaving the bedroom and when she went outside was mildly surprised because her father had the lights lit.

But of course there was no moon tonight and she'd been in her room long enough for it to get dark out.

Mike studied her over a plate of stew and softly smiled. He frequently told her she looked like her mother. He did again, right then, but he also said, "Old Weatherby'd never have to be ashamed of a daughter-in-law like you, Marty. Hell; look at those pale-eyed, bleached out women at the estates. They'd turn a man's stomach. You got 'em beat four to the mile." He nodded. "Young Andrew's got good eyesight anyway."

As though that were a cue Andrew's car-lights swung against the house from out back. She ran to peck Mike on the cheek and rush outside.

Andrew held the car door for her looking appreciative but unsmiling. He'd scrubbed his hands but that kind of grease simply did not yield. His clothing was fresh and clean. He looked darker in the face than she was and when he bent to brush her lips his hair smelled good.

"Lambs to the slaughter," he mumbled, turning the car. "You aren't afraid are you?"

She hadn't really analysed her own feelings. She'd been thinking of all the others. She was afraid all right; she knew it the moment she looked inward. But what she said was: "I don't see how old John and Miss Moody could get your father to go with them tonight. After all, they don't even work for him any longer."

Andy turned. "Never underestimate the power of a woman — or a Texan." He smiled.

She smiled back and relaxed a little. When he didn't look quite so grim it was easier for her to face the improbables towards which they were driving.

"Did you do any work after I left?" she asked.

"Well; I tried getting my hands clean in the river," he replied. "But otherwise I just stood around like a fat banker admiring the corded-up racks of wood. You know, Marty, I never before owned a commodity — something tangible I could sell."

"You like the feeling?"

"Next to making love to you I can't imagine a better feeling."

They cut across the main arterial roadway and took a side-street to get into the centre of town. There were rows of orange-lighted windows up here, a few strollers out in the night, sounds and scents of civilization that also got audible the closer they got to the main thoroughfare where autos and trucks added to the scene.

They turned northward at the first intersection which happened to also be the corner upon which sat John Richards' dowdy little hotel. Andy looked but caught no sight of John. He didn't act as though he'd expected to.

Where they passed the theatre a little queue was already lining up — school-kids who had to get right home after the first feature in order to get to bed on time because tomorrow was a schoolday.

They cruised down the roadway with nothing to say to each other until, out farther, they could see the little juice-stand and café which was their destination. There were no other automobiles out there. The same thought crossed both minds: Either John and Rachel had failed with their plan, or else it was too early for Andy's father to show up yet.

Martha said candidly, "I'm relieved, Andy."

He nodded, wheeling into the parking area. "Are you hungry?"

She shook her head, alighted, smoothed down her dress and cast an anxious look back towards town. There were no approaching headlights. He came round, took her arm and lightly steered her around front and inside where a fading blonde woman beamed upon them. They were evidently her first customers.

They ordered food, not very much of it, and Andy had to go to the water-cooler to re-fill his glass three times. The last time the waitress made a joke about it. She also stood gazing out the window, then turned to call back to someone in the kitchen.

"It's beginning. Here's another car."

Andy and Martha twisted to also see out the window. They recognized his father's Lincoln where it eased almost without sound beneath a light suspended from a tree limb out front. Martha took in a big breath then let it out very slowly. Three people alighted, two were tall men, one was a small, stocky woman.

Andy at least stopped toying with his food. Martha watched him begin to eat as though he were hungry. He winked at her. They both turned forward acting as though all this was a surprise to them.

Lynne Weatherby was wearing a tan cardigan despite the night's warmth, his shirt-collar was open and he had loafers on his feet, plus an old comfortable pair of flannel slacks. He held the door for Rachel to pass inside first, then walked in behind her leaving John to come last.

Because he was no dilettante in any undertaking, he walked straight over to the table. With a not-unkindly glance he said, "Good evening, young lady," then spun a chair from another table, straddled it and looked squarely at his son. Rachel and John went over by the water-cooler to have some water, which was perhaps less feigned on this warm night than it might have looked.

Martha saw them looking at her. She put aside her napkin but Andy guessed she was preparing to leave the table and said, "Stay, Marty." He then leaned back slightly to gaze at his father. "We'll be married in September." He didn't say it loudly nor defiantly. It wasn't an ultimatum; it was a statement of fact.

Lynne Weatherby puffed out his cheeks. He

seemed to have a comment to make, but he was learning what it was to be a prospective father-in-law. He might not approve of his son's choice at all, but there was another factor: If he ever said anything to that effect before either his son or the girl — and later on they *did* get married — he'd have sowed the seeds of something none of them would ever forget.

He turned as the waitress came. "Coffee, please." When she departed he said, "Fine; September's a fine month. June is better — so I'm told — but September will do as well. What about school, Andy?"

"I'm not going back."

A little vein in the side of Lynne Weatherby's neck swelled. "Not going back, eh? Andy; you've been going to school since you were in knee-pants. It's all been leading up to this last semester. You're throwing it all away."

"That'll be up to me, Dad."

Now the vein throbbed noticeably but otherwise it was difficult to tell from Lynne Weatherby's expression what his thoughts were, or his mood.

Martha said, speaking in a small voice, "Mister Weatherby; at least you and I agree on one thing."

Weatherby turned, dropped his pale gaze to her dark eyes briefly, then turned back towards his son again.

"I've hired old John back," he said.

Andy was like stone. "You couldn't have replaced him anyway."

Blue eyes locked with blue eyes. Lynne Weatherby was taller than his son but nowhere nearly as broad. Still, they resembled one another very much. Weatherby accepted the coffee the waitress brought. She went across to the table where John and Rachel had seated themselves.

"Do you want a pound of flesh?" the father asked his son.

Andy glanced at Martha. She was scarcely breathing. He seemed to be considering her too, until he spoke, then clearly he'd reverted to an earlier idea that this was strictly between his father and himself.

"All I want is to be left alone," he said.

Chapter Eleven

Lynne Weatherby sipped coffee and thought. He'd made concessions; actually he'd held himself in check rather well considering that he was neither a very tolerant nor patient man.

"You're not going back to college," he said, gazing into his coffee-cup. "And you want to go on being a woodcutter."

"What's wrong with that?" challenged Andrew.

"Nothing, Andy. As a matter of fact I didn't start out very differently myself. But I didn't get married until I had a little capital ahead to use towards making more capital." The blue eyes came up swiftly, stabbing towards Andrew. "You've got plenty of examples around Carleton, son; look at the boys who've rushed right out of high school or college and got married. In the first place it takes everything they can make to support a wife — but children come. Carleton's full of them; young men with promise who've got to scrape and save just to pay the bills. They'll never have enough money to grow on."

There were such examples and in fact Andy had known several of them, had attended high school with them, so he knew what his father had said was true. But he didn't place himself in that category either so he said, "Just let me make my own mistakes, Dad. I appreciate you mean well. You're probably right too, but I've been on my own a week now and I like the idea. The longer I'm on my own the better I like it."

Lynne Weatherby finished his coffee, looked round where Rachel and John were eating, straightened on his chair and looked at Martha. "I want you to know something, young lady. I have no personal aversion to you. I've made a point of seeing you before. You are very pretty and I'm told by those who know you around town you're practical and sensible. If those things are true I think you'll understand what I want is what's best for Andy."

Martha nodded. She felt miserable. She thought Mister Weatherby was behaving very well. It was Andy who was being disagreeable.

Weatherby paused, glanced at their plates of scarcely-touched food and started to arise. "Well; we've had words, Andy, but maybe it's as John said. Love is always a stranger." He stood.

Andy was perplexed. "What does that mean — love is a stranger?"

Weatherby looked round where John was, looked back and explained. "John said when a man's child falls in love it's like a total stranger has come into the house. Think about it. I have;

in fact I thought about it most of the day while I was in the city. It makes a lot of sense. *John* makes a lot of sense. Of course that's why I hired him years ago. But what I *didn't* hire him for was the influence he's had over you. I'm sorry about that, but it's done."

"Why did you hire him back, if you disapprove of him?"

"I don't disapprove of old John, son. And the reason I hired him back was to have someone on *my* side." Lynne Weatherby glanced for the last time at Martha. "I wonder if you'd do me a favour, young lady?"

"If I can," she murmured, forcing her eyes to meet his.

"Come and see me one of these days."

Andrew stiffened; both Martha and his father saw it. Martha, fearful what Andy might blurt out, said she'd come and see Mister Weatherby as soon as she could.

He paced across to the counter, dropped several paper dollars on the formica top, said that was to pay for everything, went back and asked if John and Rachel wished to drive back with him. They declined so he walked out of the café alone.

For ten seconds the little room was totally quiet, then John's chair scraped as he arose to move closer to Andy's table. Rachel didn't leave her supper; she went on eating as though there was nothing else on her mind.

John dropped down upon the chair Andy's father had vacated, shot a look around then said,

"Well; 'don't know that this did a whole lot of good but it seemed to clear the air a mite."

Andy's temper was still up. "Don't do it again, John. I realize you and Rachel meant well, but I'll tell you about what I told *him*. Don't butt into my life."

Martha fidgeted but John was unperturbed. "Sure not," he agreed amiably. "The thing was, Andy, while most talk is just so much wind, when a couple fellers got a real difference it never hurts to sort of hack a little back and forth. And I thought your pappy kept control right well, too."

Rachel arose and came over to tap John on the shoulder. She had long since figured out that Andy hadn't been surprised to see them. She'd also guessed why. She shot Martha a faintly flustered look and said, "If he's going to be working tomorrow you'd best get him home. A man's got to have his rest when he's doing manual labour." She tapped John a little harder on the shoulder. He arose.

Martha said, "We'll drive you back," but old John shook his head, smiling down into her lifted face.

"Naw. It's a real pleasant night for walkin' and it's only a little distance anyway." He reached, patted Andy roughly and turned to take Rachel's arm and steer her out of the café.

It was all over.

Martha slumped. For a moment they didn't look at one another. Andy seemed embarrassed; acted as though he wasn't proud of the part he'd played. She was going to gently remonstrate but thought better of it. She hadn't forgotten that little remark he'd made about nagging. But if he gave her an opening she'd tell him what she thought.

He didn't give her the chance. He rummaged for change but the waitress said his father had paid so he left a tip and got up. Martha walked out into the night with him and felt much better the moment she could see the crisp, white stars and the dark sky. There were lights southward where the centre of town lay. There was an occasional sound from down there as well.

He held the door for her, then closed it and leaned down studying her face. "I guess I could have acted differently. When I've been through as much unpleasantness as *he* has I'll be able to. Right now. . . . Sometimes twenty seems awfully old, other times it makes you feel like a little kid, doesn't it?"

She smiled up at him saying nothing.

They drove back the way they'd come as far as the movie house. He asked if she'd like to see the picture. She demurred using as her excuse what Rachel had said about him getting his rest. Actually, she couldn't have concentrated on the picture anyway.

When they eased down towards the creek past the tall poplars, he cut the lights and coasted in behind her house so as not to arouse Mike, then he twisted from under the wheel, threw an arm across the back of the seat and said, on thinking it over, it hadn't been a wise thing to have that meeting.

She only commented on the fact that it would have come sooner or later, and controlled an urge to say more.

"Well; it sure ruined an evening," he said ruefully, and reached to turn her face.

They kissed. She had a lump in her throat. Before things got out of hand she mentioned something which had occurred to her earlier, when she'd been up at the wood-lot with him.

"If you'll bring your laundry down, Andy, I'll do it for you."

He gave her that little quirked-up smile he'd shown before when she'd spoken of irrelevant things when they'd been making love. "I might do that, Marty. It wouldn't hurt for you to get in practice would it?"

She didn't need the practice. She'd been doing laundry for years. She leaned her head back upon the seat to gaze upwards. There were some paper-thin drifting clouds up there, so diaphanous stars shone right through them. It was a beautiful night, and yet it also hinted to her that summer was coming to a close.

"Five weeks," she murmured, rolling her head to gaze at him. "That isn't very long, Andy."

His little smile lingered, but there was a thoughtful cast to his glance. "You know, it isn't necessary to have children right away, Marty. What my father said was right. You know the couples as well as I do who live in town and barely make it from week to week."

She knew them, and she hadn't planned on starting a family at once so she said, "We'll get along, Andy. I can get a job too, if I have to."

He was opposed to that but they didn't argue over it. He moved closer and put a calloused palm upon her throat where a steady pulse beat. It quickened at his touch. "Rachel and John meant well."

She nodded.

"I'm not very surprised my dad hired John back."

"What about Rachel Moody?"

He didn't know and his thoughts were mixed. "I've known her most of my life. If he tried to get her back too she won't go until she's darned good and ready. You know how stubborn Yankee New Englanders are."

She smiled into his eyes. She knew all right.

They kissed softly. He used the hand on her throat to tilt up her face a little. It was a sweet kiss and she made no move to free herself. Afterwards, with the little pulse beating harder, he said he'd better be getting along, that on the morrow he expected to complete cutting through to the old country road which would make it easier for him to bring in supplies such as fuel and food.

She moved sluggishly. It was very pleasant in the car this warm night. When she alighted he also got out. They met in front of the car and strolled towards the sagging front porch. He said it might not be a bad idea if they began house-hunting, that if she'd like he wouldn't work the following Friday and they could go together.

She thought it was a little early for that but agreed to go with him on the following Friday. She also wondered about the details of getting married. They were required by law, she thought, to have some kind of health check and buy a licence at the Court House. He suggested she find out about those things and reached to hold her two hands out front of the house.

"It just didn't seem it would ever get this close, Marty. All the frustrations. . . ."

"You can still back out, Andy."

He gave a rough tug pulling her up against him. "That works both ways, love."

"No," she whispered, raising on tiptoes to meet his mouth, then dropping back down. "That's something I couldn't do even if I had to."

He left. She stood on the dark porch looking after him. She stood out there in the warmth until his car was only an echo heading back up towards the country road, then she didn't go into the house but strolled down by the boat and sat on a stump down there watching oily dark water move past.

It was hard to know what to do almost any time a problem arose, but it was a lot harder when one's heart interfered with one's mind. She thought she knew what Mister Weatherby would want to speak with her about: Andy finishing school; the pair of them waiting until a better time to get married; perhaps even trying to convince her the marriage would be a tragic mistake.

She too had misgivings, but at least she was resolved about making every possible effort to make the marriage a success. She knew, somehow — instinctively she told herself — that successful marriages are more often made by women than by the men-partners.

She thought back to what little she remembered of her mother and tried to guess what thought had gone through her mother's mind during those long, frustrating years in shantytown watching life turn Martha's father into a drinker, a sly and defensive man.

Of course Martha wouldn't have those troubles because Andy had iron in his spirit. But she didn't delude herself; there would be other dilemmas. She even felt saddened and slightly demoralized that they'd be starting their wedded life under the cloud of his father's disapproval; that there would be that difference in environments.

She left the stump, finally, heading for the house. She was tired. It hadn't been a hard day, physically, but emotionally it had drained her. She stopped a hundred feet off and looked critically at the house with its rotting porch, its sagging roofline, its smelly lobster boxes hanging here and there. It wouldn't be hard to leave it but she'd never forget it either. Regardless of what others thought of her father he'd always been kind and good to her. She was aware of the fact that he'd been a failure but he was still her father. She loved him. Even his drinking, although she strongly disapproved, didn't detract from her affection for him.

It suddenly occurred to her that he *hadn't* been a failure. After her mother's death he'd devoted his life to her. He'd never allowed her to sulk or mope; he'd taken her with him every chance he got. He'd given her all he'd been able to give.

She bit her lip, ran silently on through to her bedroom, sank face-down upon the pillows and cried. She didn't know why she cried; didn't really care but it was an enormous relief to do it.

Chapter Twelve

Andy came by the following evening, had supper with Martha and Mike, then the two of them left Mike on the porch smoking and went for a walk down towards the river, which was southeasterly from the creek.

A little moon was hanging up there in a black setting with stars teasing it all round. For a while, earlier in the day there'd been drifting clouds as though it might get sultry and rain, but it had cleared in late afternoon.

Andy said the heat had been bad because there wasn't a breath of air stirring up where he'd been cutting. She understood about that. There were days in summertime New England when it was hard to breathe. Not very many, but that only made them more noticeable when they appeared.

He left early that night because he had to go into town before the stores closed and get more supplies. She said she might row up and visit the next day — but she didn't do it.

Instead, because it had been preying on her

mind, she decided to go see his father. She viewed that as she'd viewed the prospect of taking medicine when she'd been a child. It was something one had to do, so the sooner one did it and got it over with the better.

Her father went out early with the boat and traps. She'd made him a lunch and filled his thermos with tart lemonade; the best thing, he'd taught her, for a fisherman to take out with him when he wouldn't be able to drink a lot of water for fear of heat-stroke, or dehydration from perspiring too much.

She took the old car and drove as straight as she could to the Weatherby estate. At the wrought-iron gates where there was a little metal call-box up to the house, she had her first serious misgivings. But Mister Weatherby had asked *her* to call; she wasn't coming as a supplicant to ask *him* favours.

The voice from the house belonged to Vichter. Moments after she'd identified herself the gate swung noiselessly open; she piled back into the old car and drove through.

She was very conscious — painfully so in fact — of the incongruity of her father's old automobile rolling up through those spacious grounds, landscaped so beautifully. Even the macadam she was driving over wasn't black like most asphalt road-toppings. It'd had cement dusted over it years back when it had been new. Mighty rollers had then ground that into the surface giving a silvery appearance.

The house was a half mile or better from the gate. Everything, she thought as she drove resolutely along, had been engineered to impress, and it succeeded. Too well, she told herself; by the time she began the big curve which ended out front of the fieldstone mansion, she felt as though she'd been robbed of dignity, pride, even her personality. She pitied anyone coming here to see Lynne Weatherby seeking favours. They'd be broken in spirit before they ever switched off the engine.

She didn't know Harry Vichter, who was standing on the long flagstone verandah waiting for her, but his short white jacket told her he was a servitor. She left the car, gave the door an unnecessarily hard slam, smoothed her skirt and marched straight ahead refusing to even look up at the second storey or at the flourishing high shrubs that dwarfed her.

Movement to one side over near a cultivated big bed of tree-roses caught her attention. Old John Richards stepped forth, shirt dark with honest sweat, and gave her a slow, warm smile. She stopped, sagged a little and smiled back. John jerked his head for her to go on. He raised a bony brown fist and gently shook it towards the house as though to tell her to give 'im hell. She felt a lot better.

Harry Vichter's face was smoothed out into an expressionless look but his eyes showed curiosity. He knew who she was obviously, but she was certain she'd never seen him before.

"Mister Weatherby'll be right down," he said, closing the door soundlessly behind her. "If you'll come through here into the sitting-room. . . ."

She saw the picture over the mantel at once, thought of the picture her father kept atop the cupboard and for a moment reflected on how strange it was both she and Andy were motherless.

Harry stopped by a huge arched window looking down across the acreage towards the front gate, adjusted a drape, smoothed several heavy pleats then looked askance at Martha. She was conscious of his presence all the while she was examining the room. She'd never seen one like it, not even in magazine illustrations. She thought a fortune had gone into creating just this one room. If there were other rooms equally as grand, then the Weatherbys must have an awesome amount of money tied up in just the house.

She turned, looked squarely at Vichter, and he at once became very busy with a tassel which hung suspended near one of the drapes. Finally, she heard footfalls. Vichter heard them too and hastily departed without making a sound.

Andrew's father had a paisley scarf under his collar. He was wearing tennis shoes and the same grey flannel trousers he'd worn the night before, but today he also was in a short-sleeved shirt. He looked tanned and fit. He even looked friendly, which was an enormous relief, as he came in out of the entry-way smiling at her.

"I've been batting a few," he said, and since he didn't explain she assumed he thought she ought to know what that meant. She vaguely thought he might be referring to baseball, but that didn't make much sense, a man his age batting baseballs.

"Andy's been beating me for the past two years. It's very demoralizing, so I'm taking advantage of his — outing — to get in a lot of practice. By the way; are you any good at tennis, Martha?"

She'd played a little at high school. "No, I'm afraid not," she murmured as he led her to a chair and asked if he couldn't get her something — ice-cream perhaps, since it was such a scorcher out.

She smiled. She knew exactly what he was doing and was grateful to him for it. He knew she was un-nerved, frightened and apprehensive. He was very easily and gently putting her at ease. He even dragged a chair across the inches-deep carpeting and sat down closer. Then he leaned back, eyed her and said, "Well." She got the impression he was as much at a loss for words as she was, and that was reassuring too. It made it a lot easier to find him human.

She took her courage in hand and said, "Mister Weatherby; I know you want Andy to finish school. I also want him to. But — please — don't you think it's really up to him? What I'm trying to say is — maybe you and I know what *we* think is best for him — and maybe we're right. I

120

really think we are. But all we're going to do by insisting is get him more set against us as well as against going back."

He conceded that point without a sound by simply bobbing his head a little solemnly as he sat studying her.

"And the wood-cutting," she plunged on, encouraged by his acquiescence on the first score. "I know you planned better things for him. In the city, perhaps. But couldn't he start out cutting wood — start out working with his hands like a lot of other men have done?"

"Definitely," said Lynne Weatherby, which left Martha bracing into a stone wall that wasn't there at all.

"Well," she said, floundering.

"Well, young lady, what I'd really like to know is — do you love my son all that much?"

She felt his eyes appraising her. She also felt her colour creeping forth. "All that much," she said, and gravely inclined her head.

"Did he tell you that in the course of our argument when he left home that he didn't want to inherit from me?"

"No," said Martha honestly. "I didn't ask about that argument and he only told me part of it. Whether he inherits anything from you or not isn't as important as you coming to see — him — after we're married, Mister Weatherby." She leaned a little. "You may be angry at him now, but please get over it before next month, Mister Weatherby. I know he acts tough, but if you

121

weren't at the wedding it would hurt him."

"I'll be there, young lady, but of course I'll have to be invited."

She straightened back. "You'll be the first one to get an invitation. I'll see to that myself."

"Thank you." Lynne Weatherby smiled at her. He was a handsome, very distinguished-looking man. When he smiled she forgot to be afraid of him. "Now would you tell me, young lady, what your father thinks of all this?"

She wasn't sure what he meant but took a plunge anyway. "He only knows Andy is on his own. Neither your son nor I have told him there was any — unpleasantness."

"I see. You don't take your father into your confidence either, eh?"

"Yes. My father is very good to me. But I have my own life to live."

Weatherby's eyes narrowed just the slightest bit. "I see," he said. "In other words your father doesn't butt into your affairs as I do into my son's affairs."

She bit her lip, held it a moment then released it. "I didn't mean it to sound like that at all."

"I apologize for taking it that way," he said, stood up and held out a hand. "Come along. I need some ice-cream whether you do or not. We can talk in the kitchen if you don't mind."

She didn't mind, and she also had a bowl of ice-cream. But she was troubled by something. She knew she'd be no match at all for Lynne Weatherby if this were a matching of wits, but he was so suave, so charming and so disarming, she was prepared to believe he wasn't trying to trap her, and that's what bothered her. Because he *was* so suave she couldn't make up her mind about him.

He asked her if she knew how to lay lobster traps. She replied that she'd been setting them out since she'd been twelve years of age. He said that as a youth in Maine he'd done the same thing with his father. He then asked her if she had any idea how married life was at the outset. She said she was used to hardships; she knew *she'd* make out all right, and she prayed every night Andy would too.

He asked other questions — things about her father, about her dead mother, even about her quitting school, which made Martha very uneasy because it meant he'd been investigating her, for otherwise he wouldn't have known she'd quit school.

She answered each question with absolute candour even though — as with quitting school — she'd had to admit it was primarily because she didn't have enough acceptable clothing, a fact other girls didn't let her forget.

They had another bowl of ice-cream; Lynne Weatherby ate in silence for a while. "You know, what Richards and Moody tried to do yesterday was very kind." The frosty eyes came up slowly to rest upon her face. "But perhaps you're right; perhaps we ought to all just leave Andrew alone."

She nodded without verbally agreeing, finished

the ice-cream and put the bowl aside. The kitchen was reached by going through a huge butler's pantry, and it was a very large, immaculate room. They were sitting at the same table Rachel had been seated at the night she'd had words with Mister Weatherby and had quit. Martha knew none of this, although she said, "Mister Weatherby; haven't you got anyone to do the cooking since Miss Moody left?"

He looked at her gravely. "I've been going into town for my meals." He grimaced. "They can't cook in Carleton any better than they can cook in Maine."

Martha drew in a breath. "Why not hire Miss Moody back?"

"She won't come."

"Well; but John Richards did. Maybe she'll — "

"For your information, young lady, I called her this morning, where she's staying. She told me she'd come back the day I agreed to hold the wedding reception here after you and Andrew are married."

Martha was flabbergasted and showed it. She was also flustered so she arose from the table, said she was grateful for the ice-cream, it was delicious, and started out of the kitchen.

Lynne Weatherby followed her as far as the entry hall. There he reached, caught hold of her arm and turned her towards him.

"I'm going to agree," he said. "Martha; I'm not saying I've been wrong. I'm not all convinced that I have been. But I'm going to do exactly as my son ordered me to do, and as you have suggested that I do. I'm not going to interfere in his life at all. Stand or fall, from here on he'll do it strictly on his own." He squinted a little at her. "Does that please you?"

She reached and impulsively took his hand, squeezed it and dropped it. "Very much, Mister Weatherby. Is it all right if I tell Andy?"

"I hope you do. And — well — maybe if the pair of you have a free minute some evening you might drop by. Could you manage that, do you suppose?"

She smiled at him. "I'll bring him, Mister Weatherby. Good-bye."

"Good-bye, Martha."

Chapter Thirteen

It had all been too easy, too pleasant. She recalled the bad things she'd heard about Lynne Weatherby and while in fact they were actually only spiteful things said by people around the village who wouldn't have been able to know him, she kept them in mind because the more she thought of it, the more she became convinced he was up to something. He *had* to be. Otherwise Andy's predicament didn't make a whole lot of sense.

She drove home, left the car in tree-shade and walked round to the porch and sat down. She *wanted* to believe Mister Weatherby was contrite. That he truly meant what he'd said back there. But he'd never once got angry or argued with her, or denounced Andy's stubbornness. He hadn't actually said a whole lot about Andy at all. He'd spoken mostly of her; had asked questions, had worked at ingrating himself, and had thoroughly charmed her.

She went back in her mind to everything that

had been said since she'd first entered the house trying to recall the shadings of words, his expressions, her own impressions.

She came up with nothing sinister. She even tried imagining a number of reasons why he'd have done such an about-face and except for getting Andy back, couldn't see what ulterior purpose he'd have had, because he most certainly hadn't acted as though he disapproved of her, which she'd gone to his estate expecting to see.

She arose, finally, when she thought her father might be coming, went indoors and began preparing the evening meal even though it was still daylight outside. Working with mechanical movements she decided Lynne Weatherby *hadn't* just charmed her, hadn't pumped her for all the information he could get because he had some scheme of his own he wished to implement. She told herself he'd behaved perfectly the night before at the café and he'd acted the same way today, and since she knew town-gossip never was truthful anyway, she was being dishonest to him and unfair to herself to keep looking for something to distrust him about.

She decided to take him entirely at his word.

Later, when her father returned, she went out to help him put the catch into brine-barrels. She didn't mention going to the Weatherby estate and he was too engrossed with the work to ask what she'd done anyway.

Even after he'd cleaned up and had a shot of rye whiskey before supper, telling her he hadn't heard the saw up above "salt spit," he still over-looked what she might have encountered this day.

She was interested that he hadn't heard the saw. "Maybe it was lunch time," she said.

"Well; I did stop alongside the bank above the old hotel a half mile or so to eat," said her father. "But when that was done with I trowled back and forth for another hour, then started for home, so I was up there most of the afternoon, and never once did I hear the saw."

She wondered. "Perhaps it broke down. He's been using it awfully hard."

Her father agreed. He finished his whiskey, went to the table and sat, then he blew out a big breath and said it was about as hot a day as he could remember.

They ate with fireflies outside in the dusk and dratted little gnats inside flying frantically round the light bulb. There were good screens on the windows. That was mandatory in summertime New England; otherwise mosquitoes ate a person alive, but there were millions of gnats so small they came right through a screen. They didn't bite nor actually bother except that unless the butter were kept covered they'd land on it; annoyances like that.

Mike was tired. He also looked dried out, which happened frequently in summertime when fishermen spent the entire day upon the water under a pitiless sun. When they'd finished supper he made no effort to drive up to one of the taverns. That let his daughter know he had indeed put in a wearying day. He retired very early and Martha was still cleaning up from supper when the car-lights swung past the sink-window raking along the upper reaches of the creek. She knew it was Andy without bothering to listen for the sound of his car.

She hastened a little, finished, dried her hands and went outside. He was striding forward and didn't see her at once. He had both hands pushed deep into trousers pockets, his head down as he walked. She thought he must be very tired too, until she recalled what her father had said about the saw being quiet this afternoon.

He looked up, sighted her and didn't smile as he moved on up. She asked if he'd eaten. He said he had, in town. She led him to one of the rickety porch chairs and he sprawled in it looking down where darkness hid the creek but could not hide its sounds.

"End of the world today," he said dully, without looking round where she sat.

"Something happened to the saw, didn't it? Dad was up there on the river and told me he didn't hear it. What happened?"

He pushed out his legs. "Not the saw," he said. "Someone bought the hotel property."

The implication, or perhaps it was the dead tone he used, made her heart skip a beat. "Bought the property . . . ?"

"Yeah." He turned his head. Even in the darkness his eyes shone with dullness she'd never seen in them before. "It's been tax-deeded to the county for years. That's common knowledge. They've been trying to get it back on the active rolls so someone would pay taxes on it, but of course no one around here wanted it, and even outsiders, since they couldn't even drive to it, weren't interested."

She gave a little start. "You mean — after you've opened the road . . . ?"

He didn't know. "All I can say with any certainty is that a fellow came up where I was cutting this morning and served notice for me to desist and said that the property had been redeemed from the county and was now private land."

"Who was he?"

Andy didn't know. "Stranger to me. He wasn't disagreeable; he just said he represented the owner and there was to be no more wood cut off the land."

Martha was struck dumb. All their hopes and plans turned to nothing so suddenly and unexpectedly left her stunned. She started to say something, checked herself and looked at Andy's profile. It was bleak in the shadows, haggard and defeated-looking. She made a heroic effort to overcome the numbness, to rescue him from the black despair which seemed to possess him. It would do no good for both of them to sit there like he was doing.

"But there's quite a bit of wood racked up isn't there?" she said, forcing her voice to be natural.

"Quite a bit," he echoed. "Five or six hundred dollars worth, Marty, but that was only the beginning."

"Well; you can keep that can't you?"

"Yes. As I said, the fellow wasn't disagreeable at all. He stood around and talked for an hour. He didn't say who'd bought the property nor why they wouldn't want the wood cut off it. He walked among the ricks and said I must've been working pretty hard to get that much bucked up. He said he was sure it'd be all right to leave the wood there until I could get it sold this autumn."

She strove to find an alternative and came up with something tentative. "Andy; there are other pieces of woodland. The north country is full of them."

He wasn't moved by this. He said it would take a week to run down the owners by going over the tax records at the Court House. He also said by the time he got another worthwhile location, even if the owner didn't want a tier out of every cord he'd cut, it would be too late.

"It takes hot weather to dry the wood, otherwise it doesn't burn well."

She felt the defeat closing in again and kept struggling against it. She told him where she'd gone and he listened but not with much enthusiasm even when she told him his father hadn't seemed at all antagonistic towards her.

All he said was: "Maybe it's a good thing because if I can't figure a way out of this other mess, I may have to go back home."

She knew how deep his demoralization was when he said that. She thought of their wedding and a cold fear settled in her breast. She tried hard to think of something soothing to say and failed utterly. Finally, she said she had lemonade in the refrigerator and went indoors. There was lemonade all right but what she needed badly was a moment alone to fight back the scald of tears that threatened.

She remembered something he'd said about having some kind of permit from the county. That gave her spirits a badly needed boost. She got the lemonade pitcher, two glasses and hastened back outside.

He accepted the glass and watched dully as she filled it. She waited a moment before mentioning the permit. His answer cut across the words before she'd finished speaking.

"That's the hell of it, Marty. I told this fellow about the agreement with the county. He said he knew all about it; that it didn't constitute anything more than a right for me to cut wood on the property until the county sold it, and since they'd sold it, I no longer had a right to cut." He looked over the rim of his glass at her. She hadn't tasted the lemonade yet. She was a little indignant.

"But that's not right, Andy. You asked for the permit, and they gave it to you, believing you'd be able to cut all the wood you wanted, up there."

He wasn't pleased by her logic at all. "Sure,

love. I know exactly what *I* had in mind, and I know what *they* had in mind. But something came along to change it all. That permit isn't a lease; I've had enough business law in college to know what'll happen if I try to make the county or this new owner let me go on cutting. They'll go to court and I'll lose."

She sipped lemonade, thought, then said, "Can't you find out who bought the property, then go ask him if he wouldn't like the timber and underbrush cleared off?"

He nodded. "That's what occurred to me after I got over the shock. By then that fellow had gone so I suppose tomorrow I'll have to go over to the tax office and look up the new owner on the rolls — if he's listed there. Anyway; someone'll know who he is. And you're right. That's our best move." He finished the lemonade looking better than he'd looked earlier. He didn't smile but he said, "I think I know what it's like to be shot. First, you're too stunned to believe it could happen. Then you're scairt. The last thing you do is begin to think of ways to get your health back." He held out the glass, she re-filled it. "But from what the fellow said today I'm not very hopeful. He said the new owner didn't want the trees destroyed. When I showed him there was no way to reach the property until more right-of-way had been cleared he just said his orders were to stop the sawing. That's all he knew."

Martha, past the shock now, said thoughtfully, "But who in the world would buy that property;

the hotel's past salvaging, my father says, and the land actually is nothing but jungle."

Andrew had no idea although he pointed out to her that there was an ideal boating site up there, and that even though the old hotel was beyond saving, where it sat, up the long slope from the Pawtucket, would make a beautiful place for a home.

"Probably someone from the city bought it," he said. "Maybe to develop it into an estate. He won't be the first one to discover Carleton. My parents did about the same thing twenty years or so ago. All these other estates around Carleton were once run-down farms or resorts."

She mutely agreed with all this but that wasn't what held her attention. His father could help; he had wealth and power and influence. She didn't mention this though; if it ever came out at all Andy would have to think of it himself. She doubted that he would mention it although she was confident he'd think of it.

As though he'd read her mind he said, "Well, Marty, I said I wanted to be on my own — to make my own mistakes. I guess today I just saw where I made my first one. I never should have settled for that permit. I should have insisted on a lease of the land with the county."

Finally, he smiled. It wasn't the usual boyish expression of pleasure, it was instead a kind of wry, hard smile, but it told her that he wasn't as defeated as he'd sounded earlier, which helped her own demoralization considerably.

He finished his second glass of lemonade then said he'd be getting back to the hotel where his camp was. She walked round to the car with him. He almost forgot to kiss her. After that he stroked her hair and said, "You'll worry. That's natural, Marty. But don't give up. I haven't. I almost did, but we're going to be married next month come hell or high water — or some fellow from the city. We'll work out of this. Maybe things were going too well for us anyway. Maybe we needed this."

She snuggled against his chest. "Yes," she whispered, "we needed this like we need hemlock in the lemonade."

He laughed, got into the car and shook his head at her. "Without you I'm not sure I wouldn't just toss in the sponge. But with you, Marty, there's not a chance of me doing it now."

Chapter Fourteen

She worried all the following day. She told her father at breakfast and although he was surprised, he had no advice to offer except one philosophical remark about life knocking folks down every time they tried to get up.

She seriously considered going to see Mister Weatherby. There were two reasons she didn't. One of them was that when she drove into town to do her marketing she saw his Lincoln cruise past bound for the turnpike which led down towards New York City. She didn't actually see him in the car although she recognized Vichter driving. Nonetheless she was sure he'd been in the back seat, so there'd be no point in driving out to the Weatherby estate.

The second reason she forgot Lynne Weatherby was that when she came back to the parked auto, struggling with her box of groceries, Rachel Moody was standing there watching her progress. Rachel helped boost the box onto the rack of the car behind the front seat then said,

"You ought to make the clerks carry groceries for you, Martha. Those boxes are heavy; a person could injure their back doing things like that."

Rachel was wearing a light straw hat which sat squarely atop her head in a no-nonsense manner. Her face was pink from the heat but otherwise she looked cool enough.

"I understand you had a talk with Mister Weatherby yesterday," she said as Martha leaned in thin shade beside the old car catching her breath. "John saw you and told me."

Rachel stood primly waiting. Martha told her all that had happened. Rachel digested it impassively, looked about, saw a store that served ice-cream and, taking Martha's arm, drew her along as she said, "Mister Weatherby is a good enough man. He's always considerate — which is rare in men of his calibre. Not that they can't be considerate, mind, but they ordinarily have so many things on their minds."

Martha didn't resist being led in out of the heat. She even accepted Rachel's suggestion of a dish of vanilla ice-cream although she'd have preferred chocolate. She told the older woman of the disaster and Rachel was as unperturbed by it as Andrew could have told Martha she would have been. She said, "Well, of course Andrew will go see the new owner for additional permission," then Rachel suddenly got an odd expression up around her eyes and bent to pick up a spoon. Martha saw the odd look but it came and went so swiftly it scarcely made an impression.

They talked a little more, touched upon neutral subjects and as soon as they were finished Rachel said she had to be getting along, and left. It was a very brusque departure even for a New Englander.

Martha drove home in shimmering heat, mildly puzzled by Rachel's behaviour, and when she parked the car and saw the lanky form lift itself upright off a porch chair, she was even more puzzled. John Richards, she thought, was supposed to be at the Weatherby place working. He came out to take the box from her and carry it on into the house. For a man who had to be as old as he obviously was John was surprisingly agile, active and strong.

He said, in that quiet drawl of his, "Well; just figured I'd drop down an' see how things were going 'twixt you'n Andy."

She held the door for him to enter, pointed to the oilcloth-covered table and waited until he'd put the box down before she explained about the desist order.

John stood slightly stooped watching her without blinking until she'd told the whole story, then he strolled back out onto the porch, sought the same chair and dropped down into it. She came out too, and closed the door after herself. He scratched his mat of grizzled grey hair, pursed his lips and said, "Well, well. . . ." He didn't sound upset but the words were quieter than most words he spoke, and that, she thought, signified something. Only she didn't know old John

Richards well enough to know exactly what.

She told him about having a dish of ice-cream with Rachel, and while that should have earned only perhaps a little nod from him, he raised up a little in the chair and put a small, grey eye upon her.

" 'She say anything?" he asked.

"About what? We just talked. I told her what had happened to Andy."

"What'd she say?"

Martha recalled that sudden look of shock. But it had been such a fleeting thing she decided against mentioning it. "Not very much, Mister Richards. I suppose she was a little upset though."

" 'Ought to be," he grunted, and added nothing to it. He arose. "Well; just thought I'd come by. Better be getting back now or old Weatherby'll fire me again."

"It's a long walk," said Martha. "I'll drive you back."

"Naw. I like the walking. Anyway, I got a couple stops to make on the way. Thanks all the same. And tell Andy hello for me. I'll get up to see him one of these days." He walked off, his stride long and smooth.

She stepped to the edge of the porch looking after him. For some reason she had an odd feeling; either old John knew something about the hotel property changing hands, or else he thought Rachel did.

A crow flopped awkwardly into a tree near the

boat-landing and raucously scolded the country-side. She looked up at him. He was shiny-black and quite large. Crows sometimes nested near the creek but usually didn't come this close to the cabin.

She turned, entered the house and began putting away the groceries. She was imagining things, she told herself sternly. What could John or Rachel know about the hotel property changing hands? Andrew would come by about supper time; he'd have some answers for her.

Her father came in earlier than usual; it wasn't quite three in the afternoon in fact, and he normally didn't arrive until about five when the days were as long as they presently were.

He came to the house without any traps; she saw him coming up the path through the screen-door. He stepped onto the porch, called in to announce himself and said the boat had sprung a leak and he'd have to go uptown for some things to patch it with, then went hiking on around where the old car was.

She finished inside, then walked down to the landing. Not because she didn't believe her father, but out of curiosity. He knew every yard of the Pawtucket; she was curious to see how he'd managed to hit rocks or whatever it was that had damaged the boat.

The hole was in the side an inch or two below the waterline. She bent for close inspection. He'd hit something, but that isn't what had caused the wound; the wood was pulpy. She poked two fingers in and felt the soggy wood crumble.

She tried to remember when he'd got this boat and failed, which meant he'd had it since she'd been very small. She also tried to imagine how he could repair anything as rotten as that planking. It was discouraging; row-boats weren't actually very expensive, but when everything a man made went into just eating and clothing himself and his daughter, if row-boats had been even cheaper they'd be too expensive even then.

She went to a stump and sat, feeling sad for her father. Of course, while he was uptown, he would stop at a tavern. She didn't condemn him for it this time; she even felt as dis-spirited as she knew he'd be feeling. It must, she thought, be a terrible thing to be almost fifty years old and have no more than a man had when he was first married almost a quarter century before.

Eventually, she went back to the house to start dinner. Not that she expected her father to arrive on time, nor even to eat much if he did; he was a man who extracted every moment of forgetfulness he could from a cheap drunk. That, she thought, was also sad.

At five o'clock Andrew drove up back. She went to the door to call to him to come inside; she couldn't leave the stove. It helped her spirit having him arrive before supper. Now there'd be *someone* to sit across the table from her.

As he came in she saw that his hands were clean, that he'd evidently just come from town. He was wearing a light-coloured form-fitting cotton shirt that made his bulging muscles look even larger than they were; it also made a strong contrast with his bronze colouring.

He said, "Hi, love." Then he went over, kissed her, stepped back and said, "Well; do you want to know who bought that tax-deeded county property out from under us?"

She nodded. His expression was both triumphant and harsh.

"The New England Development Corporation," he said.

She nodded. The name meant nothing. "To fix up and re-sell I suppose."

He waited a moment. "The New England Development Corporation, Marty, is a subsidiary of the York and Westchester Bank and Trust Company of New York City."

She nodded again, but this time, seeing something cold and menacing in his eyes, said, "And . . . ?"

"And. My father is a Director of the Board of York and Westchester Bank and Trust Company." · He turned, went to the table, pulled out a chair and sank down. She felt strangely light; as though she were on the verge of heat stroke. Reaching, she felt the cool edge of the sink and leaned upon it. "Your father, Andy . . . ?"

He smiled at her. "And you told me how charming he was to you. How understanding and solicitous."

She recalled the big car going through town towards the turnpike evidently on its way to the city. She tried to think of something to say and utterly failed.

"It never crossed my mind," he muttered from half across the room, "he'd go this far."

She turned back to the stove, worked there a moment among the pans then turned to face him again. "But — it isn't worth it. Why spend all that money just to get you back home, Andy?"

He had no comment to make about that but he said, "It still won't work. I also telephoned a man in Jersey who owns a hundred acres a mile farther upriver and offered to give him one-third of my sales if he'd let me clear his land. He agreed, I got an attorney to draw up the agreement and mailed it off this afternoon."

His words dropped like steel balls into the silence. His face looked older, his eyes tougher. She thought his father would look about the same way when he was angry.

She began feeling a little better; at least Andy wasn't giving up. She remembered something he'd said about losing the hotel property might be what they needed. She repeated it but in a weak voice. He got up, crossed to the sink and got himself a drink of water. He then turned towards her.

"It'll still be September," he said harshly, and took her roughly by the arms. "I'll move up to the other piece of land tomorrow and start cutting. The attorney said it'd be better to wait until the signed Agreement came back but we can't wait — can we?"

She shook her head. His face was blurry. She kissed him, then turned aside so he wouldn't see the tears. But he felt them when her body convulsed and held her still closer.

"Don't worry; he won't be able to stop us."

"But he was so — *nice* — yesterday, Andy. We even had some ice-cream in the kitchen and . . . I don't understand it. It's too hard to believe he'd do that to us — to you."

"Forget it," he growled, and reached over to turn off the burners of the stove. "Go wash your face; we're going uptown to dinner."

"Dad'll be — "

"Never mind him either. His dinner's on the stove." He turned her, gave her a light push towards her room and said, "We'll go to the hotel dining-room tonight. We'll celebrate a defeat and a fresh start at the same time."

She went obediently and washed her face, first in warm water, then in cold. It helped her regain control, but her heart felt like lead.

She didn't want to believe the obvious. She told herself she simply couldn't have been that wrong about his father. Of course what he believed was obvious — his father had deliberately bought that parcel of property to drive him back home, back to college, and away from her.

She had to finally admit it all dove-tailed very neatly. She also had to admit Lynne Weatherby's reasons were sound, considering what he wanted for his son. And finally, she didn't really blame him too much for what he wanted, although she couldn't ever approve of the way he'd gone about it.

She dressed slowly, washed again, began to feel better and went back out into the kitchen where Andy was standing, fisted hands in pockets, studying the descending twilight through the sink window. He turned.

"You're beautiful," he said.

That made her feel a lot better. She even smiled as he held the door for her.

It was dusk out, crickets were singing and that thin little moon was overhead, fleshed out a little from what it had been the night before. She took back a deep-down breath of cooling night air and walked hand-in-hand with him to the car.

Chapter Fifteen

The following day she didn't have much time to think. Her father had come back the night before well oiled. He had arisen in the morning a little headachy but otherwise resolute. He took her down to help him with the boat. He probably could have done most of it by himself, but it required two people to block-and-tackle the craft onto the little beach next to the landing, and it also took two people to get the boat rolled over bottom-up.

After that he kept her with him for company, although he also put her to work scraping the bottom while he bored out all dowels on the rotten plank and removed it.

She told him all that had happened and while he didn't come right out in so many words and say he wasn't surprised, he left her with that impression. He also told her he'd heard uptown someone had bought that parcel of property; that the men at the bars were speculating who it'd be this time who'd make an estate on the outskirts of Carleton.

He had a steam-warped length of lumber which had been in the rafters of the dark attic for a good many years getting dry and tough, which he brought down to replace the punky piece with. She hadn't known there'd been anything up there, primarily because once as a child when she'd poked her head up into the attic out of curiosity, and had disturbed some bats, she'd been cured of ever looking up there again.

Mike explained that a man who made his living with boats was a fool if he didn't always keep an extra piece of planking around, as well as extra oar-locks, oars, and even whatever marine hardware he might need.

He also said if she'd finish stripping the bottom they might be able to get on a primer coat of white-lead this very day, which was a hint for her to work harder and worry less.

It was hot down beside the creek. They'd deliberately beached the boat where no shade would touch it. She went to the house for lemonade which her father made a face over when she offered him a glass. He was perspiring freely. By mid-afternoon he had the plank in place and ready to caulk but about then he ran out of energy, went over into the shade beneath a big tree and sat with his shoulders against the bole. She joined him but not until she'd finished scraping.

He showed her how to thump the wood for rot, then watched as she went over the little craft from bow to stern. The bottom seemed sound enough for which Mike gave thanks. She knew how to caulk and although he'd brought back a bucket of leaded oakum she sat in the shade with him instead of going back to work.

He seemed to feel better although he was lethargic; at least he was perfectly content to sit in the blessed shade and talk. He told her some of the tales he'd heard around Carleton about her prospective father-in-law. She'd heard essentially the same stories and hadn't particularly believed them. Now she listened and made no attempt to defend Lynne Weatherby. Then he said something that jangled on her nerves.

"They're saying in town he's using that woman who used to cook for him and old John Richards in his fight with Andy. 'Course, everyone knows Andy moved out and went to cutting wood for a living."

"Gossip," she said savagely. "Small people and malicious talk."

"Well maybe, Marty, but there's one thing about gossip; sometimes it's founded in fact an' you got to admit it was right about Andy."

She was going to defend Rachel and old John too, but she thought back to the odd way they'd both acted and withheld judgement about them. She liked John and she *wanted* to like Rachel Moody although she wasn't a person it was easy to like, at least not during the first phases of acquaintanceship.

"John wouldn't do anything to hurt Andy," she told her father. "They're more like father and son than Andy was with his father."

Mike had no rebuttal to offer. He finally sipped a glass of lemonade because he was dehydrated from the heat but he didn't look as though he enjoyed it very much. " 'Seems a man'd have to be doggoned mean to undercut his own son when the lad's only trying to do something on his own. But I wouldn't put it past a man like Mister Weatherby, Marty. They're a different breed from the rest of us. I've had truck with most of the estate-folk one time or another. I'm not saying I understand 'em, but I sure know they react different than I do."

She thought she knew what he was leading up to so she said, "Dad; we're still going to be married next month."

He took that in his stride. "Sure, Marty. And I'm for the both of you."

The way he said it, in a sad-sounding voice, gave her the impression he thought Andy would back out. She wouldn't let herself think like that.

"We're going to look at houses Friday," she said.

He sipped more lemonade. "I'll lose a good helper, won't I?" He smiled a trifle wanly and because she got a lump in her throat she jumped up and went back down to work on the boat.

He didn't; he continued to sit in the shade watching her for another half hour, or until the sun began to drop down beyond some distant treetops, then Andy drove in up by the house, saw them as he walked towards the porch and came down to where they were. He was wearing a sleeveless old blue shirt and his greasy dungarees. He greeted them with his boyish smile saying jokingly he liked to see Marty work because he was considering putting her to stacking wood up where he was cutting.

Mike smiled, asked how it was going, and Martha hung on Andy's answer.

"Fine. I moved up to the leased land. It's just as much a jungle as down at the hotel site. Yesterday I'd about given up getting much more wood racked up to dry this fall, but now I'm back in business. Bucked up two cords today and quit early."

All the time he'd been speaking he'd been looking straight at Martha; had been directing everything he'd said to her. She was pleased and showed it.

Mike filled a glass with lemonade and gave it to Andrew. He drank it down as though it were water and asked about the boat. They sat in the shade, he and Mike, watching Martha, talked a little about things in general until she'd finished one full seam and came over to join them, then Mike acted as though he'd suddenly remembered something and went back to the house.

Andy grinned about that. "One thing about your father," he told her. "He sure knows when three is a crowd."

She looked ruefully at her hands. Oakum made them sticky and dark. "Not very ladylike," she said.

"Ladylike enough for me," he retorted, "and that's all that matters." He tilted her head, kissed her warm mouth and lifted one coil of black hair that had tumbled across her forehead to put it back where it belonged. He was softly smiling.

"Pretty grubby pair, aren't we?" he asked, settling thick shoulders against the tree at his back. "But it's better being this way than clean like we were yesterday and down in the dumps."

She could agree with that. She could also agree with an errant thought that ran across her awareness, that he was so nice to be with when he was a little tired but satisfied.

"Is the wood as good at the new place?" she asked.

"Yes. No better but just as good."

"Is there any chance — something might happen up there too?"

He lost most of his soft smile. "I doubt it. If I can have a full week without interruptions we'll have as much wood in the new location as we have in the old one. That'll be enough to get us married and set up in a rented house." He rolled his head around. " 'Still want to go look at houses?"

She nodded, attempted to wipe the sticky material off her hands with dried grass, failed and moved to arise. "I'd better go start supper."

He caught her before she could arise. "Tell me you love me," he said, holding her.

She looked into his handsome, bronzed face. "I love you. I thought you'd be tired of hearing it by now."

151

His grip tightened; when he drew her in closer to him she came willingly. She caught the scent of wood-pitch on his clothing, the fragrance of wild lavender. She turned a little and lay her head against his shoulder. His heart was making a loud, solid sound. She stole one arm around him feeling the hard muscles.

"A month can be a very long while," she whispered, lifting her face. He nodded without comment. They sat that way until the sun dipped between two distant tall trees and shadows sprang out all around, then she worked free and stood up. "I have to go start supper. You wash up then come on inside." She held down her hands as though to pull him up. He arose without help. She probably couldn't have lifted him anyway.

The path from creekside to house wasn't very long, perhaps two hundred or two hundred and fifty feet, but they managed to make it seem like a hundred yards.

She asked if he'd heard from his father. With eyes that momentarily darkened he replied that he hadn't, and let the topic wither right there. He then asked if she'd like to see the new site where he was working. When she agreed he said he'd drive her up as far as the car could go on Friday after they'd been house-hunting, then they'd have to walk the balance of the way.

Mike was in the canvas hammock watching them approach. He told Martha her lemonade wasn't as bad as it first seemed, which of course meant his headachy sensation was gone.

Andy sat on the porch after she'd gone inside. He told Mike how much wood he had racked up in ricks of from one to three cords each, and wondered where he was going to sell it.

Mike had no idea but promised to let it be known the wood was for sale. He fished around for some way to mention Andy's father for a while then said, "I guess everyone's got to stick their oar into other folks business a little, Andy, even though they know better. I was wonderin' if it wouldn't be better to patch things up with your paw."

Andy sat like stone gazing down where the upturned boat lay. After a while in a voice that was cold he said, "How often do those row-boats get wet-rot like that?"

It was a quiet but unmistakable rebuke and Mike took it that way. He wasn't angered though, he answered the question as though that's all they'd been discussing. "Hard to say because a man tries to keep the hull painted and adequately caulked so's no dampness can get in to start the rotting process. Only in season a man's using his boat day in an' day out and has no time to really make sure, I'd say that particular rot was old; maybe two, three years. Maybe even longer."

If Mike understood how contradictory his statement had been he gave no indication. Instead, he craned to see his boat and dropped back in the hammock satisfied it hadn't moved.

"Salt-water plays hob more'n fresh water," he went on, lifting his gaze to the treetops across the creek where dusk was coming down. " 'Course where the river's so close to the ocean as it is where I trap lobsters, it's all salt-water. That's probably what hastened things."

Andy sprawled, raised heavy arms and folded them behind his head. He was listening, without heeding a thing Martha's father said. He'd accomplished his purpose, which had been to expressly switch the topic. Beyond that he didn't much care what they talked of, or even whether they talked at all. He had his own thoughts. To him they were infinitely more important than some tired little old boat.

Martha came out to see if they'd washed. Neither had so she sent them to do so. Afterwards, when they gathered round the kitchen table Andy remembered something and told them he'd seen two deer this day. Mike smiled his sly, raffish smile, saying that when Martha's mother and he had been young they'd lived the first few years before he got his fishing business under way, on illegally-killed deer.

Martha looked reprovingly at Mike. He let the subject die and drank two cups of black coffee which heightened his sense of well-being considerably. He was by this time almost entirely recovered from his drinking spree of the evening before.

It was pleasantly hot and still. Mosquitoes hummed at the screen and gnats came gliding right on through. Mike said they'd have an Indian Summer this year; that they probably wouldn't have any frost until well into November.

It happened like that now and then in New England. When it did people worried because of the very high fire danger. For the first time in her life Martha hoped very hard they wouldn't have an Indian Summer; just the thought of all that racked-up wood going up in smoke and flame sent her spirits plummeting.

Chapter Sixteen

Mike was down working on the boat and Martha was out back weeding the geranium bed when the limousine came cautiously down the rutted narrow lane. Martha saw it first and caught her breath. She didn't recognize anything but the car at first, but by the time it got close enough for her to see Harry Vichter at the wheel she knew who'd be in the rear seat, and fled around front to wash dirt from the flowerbed off hands and arms and to also brush her hair.

Mike didn't see the car at all. In fact he didn't even happen to look up when Lynne Weatherby strode down the side of the house to the porch where Martha met him, looking more presentable. She faced him without smiling and her greeting was perfunctory.

He studied her briefly, seemingly mildly bewildered by her attitude, then, when she made no offer of a chair, he took one anyway.

"I've been wondering why you haven't been to see me. Remember, you said you'd bring Andrew."

"He doesn't want to see you," she told him, still standing.

Weatherby looked up, his brows drawing inwards slightly at her tone. "Obviously something is wrong, young lady, would you tell me what it is? The last time we met you were — different."

"That time I didn't know what you'd done, Mister Weatherby."

"What I'd done . . . ?"

"Buying the old hotel property upriver so Andy'd lose his wood-cutting rights."

Weatherby gazed at Martha serenely but his eyes showed a hint of bafflement. "I haven't bought any property up the river or down the river, Martha. In fact I haven't bought any property at all in — "

"Andy told me you were some kind of director of the York and Westchester Bank and Trust Company, Mister Weatherby."

"That's true."

"And that a company called the New Engand Development Corporation is a subsidiary of the other company, Mister Weatherby."

"That is also true." Suddenly Lynne Weatherby straightened in the chair. "Are you saying New England Development bought that old hotel site up the river?"

"Mister Weatherby; if you're an officer of the bank you'd know what the development company was doing wouldn't you?"

He stood up without answering, looked down where Mike was working, his bowed back

157

towards the house, and for a moment she saw his temper. It darkened his face and pulled his mouth out long and thin and lipless. Then the mood passed, he turned and gazed down at her, eyes still smoky.

"Young lady those are two separate concerns. The bank uses the development company as a subsidiary for investment purposes only. As a member of the Board of Directors I only know what capital investments are made and what capital gains are secured. Unless I go through the entire investment folio I don't know what is being bought or developed."

"Then you didn't know about the hotel site?"

"No," he said simply and forthrightly. Then he also said, "Damn; how did they happen to hit on the one site that could cause trouble between my son and me?"

She had no answer, of course, and apparently neither did he. She kept studying him because she wanted to believe; in fact she *did* believe him.

Finally, Mike saw them up there on the porch, put aside his tools, wiped his hands on a rag and started towards the house. Weatherby saw Mike coming but paid him scant attention. He said, "Martha; where is Andrew now?"

She explained about the new lease a mile farther up-country but since she'd never been there couldn't give any very accurate description on how to reach the place. He asked if the road were adequately passable. She doubted it; Andrew had said he'd take her up there but they'd have to walk some of the way. Weatherby turned as Mike stopped just beyond the porch, and nodded. Mike nodded back, near to smiling. Otherwise though neither of them spoke to the other.

Weatherby said he'd go back uptown, get a Land Rover from a man he knew who owned one, and see if he couldn't reach the site where Andrew was working. He asked her if she'd like to come along. She was hesitant. Mike said he'd go, if Mister Weatherby wanted him to; that he knew most of that wooded country up-river having at one time or another prowled over most of it.

Weatherby nodded and turned back. But Martha still didn't know whether she'd want to be there — especially in the company of Andy's father as though she'd brought him — when the two Weatherbys met. Andy's father didn't press her at all; he took Mike and started swiftly back towards the car. He was no longer the kindly, re-laxed individual she'd known, but put her in mind now of an army officer or a policeman.

Later, she took her father's old car and went into Carleton to get some laundry soap. She ar-rived just in time to witness a somewhat startling confrontation. She knew only one of the antago-nists — Mister Weatherby.

The meeting took place outside the best hotel in town and the other man was a lean, younger man wearing woodmen's boots and an open-necked work shirt who, except for something about him — perhaps his bold gaze or his pale colouring — might have been a woodsman. She was parking across the road when Mister Weatherby hailed the younger man as the latter was strolling forth from the hotel. They knew each other, obviously, since they used one another's names. She saw her father at the side of a four-wheel-drive ugly little vehicle talking to Vichter, neither of whom saw the trouble coming before Martha did.

Weatherby called out a name bringing the younger man around towards him in obvious surprise. Martha saw the quick, hard way Mister Weatherby strode up. She caught the first sentence easily because Mister Weatherby said it loudly enough.

"Jamison; why didn't you come out to my home and tell me you were in Carleton to buy that land up the river?"

The younger man eyed Weatherby with slow-rising antagonism. "That's never been necessary before," he retorted. "It never crossed my mind this time."

Apparently Mister Weatherby didn't believe the younger man. "You knew who that wood-cutter was you ordered off the hotel site, Jamison. You knew if my son was working up there I'd be interested."

Jamison's resentment was fully up now. There were people turning to look at them along the sidewalk outside the hotel. "Mister Weatherby; company policy is to make certain once control has been gained nothing is removed from our development lands. You know that as well as I do. Sure I heard around town that was your son cutting wood out there. And I went out of my way to be nice about it when I ordered him off." Jamison's eyes hardened. "He had no right up there anyway; all he had was a brush-clearing permit."

Martha's breath caught in her throat. Lynne Weatherby doubled his hands into fists at his side. Mike and Harry Vichter were transfixed over at the kerbing, taken totally by surprise at this fierce exchange.

Lynne Weatherby said something very low, Martha didn't catch the words but she saw Jamison's shoulders stiffen a little. She wanted to run over there and stop what she thought might be coming, but a strolling couple coming from the north got there first. She recognized Rachel by the straw hat set squarely atop her head before she knew who the easy-striding raw-boned older man was with her. John Richards.

It was John, evidently experienced in these matters, who took the scene in with one glance and stepped ahead of Rachel to approach Jamison from the left side. Martha didn't hear what old John said either, but wouldn't have in any event because he never spoke loudly nor swiftly. She saw Jamison's head whip round.

By that time Harry Vichter had started forward. Harry was a thick two-hundred-pounder, not above average height but very close-coupled and formidable-looking. Jamison saw him coming too, and wilted. He shot a venomous glare at Lynne Weatherby and said, "Part of my agreement with the development company was that I wouldn't have to kow-tow to anyone from the bank in locating and buying tax-deeded land, Mister Weatherby. I know this development building a damned sight better than you or anyone else does from the bank. I also know how to preserve the natural beauty of land to be developed and re-sold. I'm going to telephone to the city and report all this."

Mister Weatherby didn't relent although his hands were no longer balled into fists. "Do that," he snapped. "You deliberately ran my son off knowing who he was. Jamison; I'm familiar with your type. Vindictive and mean. Now you go ahead and make that telephone call." He turned on his heel, jerked his head at Vichter and stamped back where the ugly little four-wheel-drive vehicle stood.

Martha alighted, stood a moment as she watched Vichter climb under the steering wheel while her father got in back beside angry Lynne Weatherby, and the Land Rover pulled away from the kerbing.

John Richards was still standing beside the man named Jamison. He too watched the Land Rover drive off. Rachel was back in the shade of an awning, watching, her face reflecting disapproval.

Martha walked across the street and Jamison, seeing her heading straight for him, turned his back on old John to face her. He looked sharp-featured and sly, up close, decidedly unpleasant, but she still thought he deserved some kind of explanation. It didn't occur to her if he'd been in Carleton more than a week he'd probably already heard the gossip.

She told Jamison her name and looked past to old John who hadn't moved but who was now watching her. Then she said, "I won't apologize for Mister Weatherby. He had reason for being upset, but you probably didn't realize what you were doing when you put Andrew off the land upriver, Mister Jamison. There's been some — unpleasantness — between Mister Weatherby and his son. You made it worse by putting Andy off the hotel land."

Jamison's lips pulled apart in a cold and contemptuous smile. "If it's because of the kid," he said, "you're butting in, I can tell you it's a waste of breath. New England Development's got deed to that land. Neither Weatherby nor his kid can do a thing about that even though the old man's on the bank Board of Directors. Our company works independently of his lousy bank, lady. I ran the kid off because I wanted him out of there. He won't be back either, no matter who his father is. As for the rest of you people — keep off that land; it's private property now."

Jamison turned as though to re-enter the hotel. Old John didn't block his passage but he drawled a tart comment at the younger man. "I guess you got a reason for dislikin' bankers, mister; I'm not too fond of them myself. But you're kind of young. You need some lessons taught you."

Jamison's eyes flamed. "Not from you, pop," he growled, waiting for whatever old John would do next.

John smiled. "Maybe not, mister. Maybe not from me — but from *life*. You keep on goin' around with that big chip on your shoulder and you'll sure get those lessons."

Jamison stood a moment regarding old John, then made a contemptuous leer and marched past into the hotel.

Martha and Rachel converged on John, who was the least upset person anywhere around. Now, the bystanders who'd been goggling, turned and began ambling away.

Rachel said, "John Richards if he'd punched you in the nose you'd have deserved it."

Richards' little eyes twinkled. "Well maybe, Rachel, but it wouldn't have been the first punch in the nose I ever got."

Martha told them of Lynne Weatherby's earlier visit down along the creek. They listened soberly and finally Rachel said, "Child; we knew who Mister Jamison was. We also knew that Andrew's father's bank owned that company. That's what's been worrying us; we thought Mister Weatherby knew about that land deal."

Martha looked at them, finally understanding why they'd acted so oddly when they'd heard the land had changed hands where the old abandoned *Carleton Hotel* stood. It was an enormous relief; not just to discover what their interest had been, but also to discover that Lynne Weatherby hadn't known anything about that acquisition.

She smiled through a blur of salt-tears. "Mister Richards; you could treat Miss Moody and me to a dish of ice-cream," she said, and Rachel smiled. It was the first time Martha had ever seen her smile. It transformed an otherwise somewhat craggily forbidding set of features into a very attractive face.

Old John hooked both their arms and turned to guide them across the road to the ice-cream parlour. Overhead, a pale yellow disc beat downward with a breathless kind of still and malevolent heat.

Chapter Seventeen

It rained the next day and Martha worried for fear Andrew would get his convertible stuck up there in the woods. The fact that he didn't was demonstrated by the fact that he came driving in shortly after noon to take her house-hunting. It wasn't Friday, but as he said, since he couldn't do much work in the rain if they went looking today, then perhaps if it didn't rain Friday he'd be able to get in a full day at the wood-lot.

He hadn't seen his father. In fact when she told him Lynne Weatherby had gone searching, with her father and that chauffeur of his father's, he was surprised. He was also astonished by what she related of the angry confrontation in town between his father and Jamison and made her describe the younger man, which she did.

"That's the one," he said. "That's the man who ordered me off the hotel site." He took her out to the car, helped her in then ran through rain to his own side and slid under the wheel. "Maybe it was a coincidence they happened to buy the hotel site, but it's hard to believe my father wouldn't have known."

She still believed his father hadn't known and said so. She also described his father's wrath when he found out what Jamison had done. They drove up to town, turned onto the main thoroughfare and cruised slowly as far as the theatre. There were several estate offices in town which might have listings of houses to let. One was beside the theatre but although Andy parked in front of the place he sat in brooding thought making no effort to alight. Eventually he turned and said, "Well; I'll think about it. Maybe I'll go see my father. But whether he knew or not, the important thing is that we've got another piece of land, so let's look at houses." He smiled. She smiled back.

They looked at houses all afternoon. There were quite a number up for rental because the season was nearly over; vacationers up from New York City were trekking back where they'd come from. One of the salesmen who showed them homes was a youth they'd both known years earlier in high school. He presumed upon this most tenuous of all friendships to make a quip about Andrew's break with his father. That was a mistake. Andrew cut him off, hard.

One house pleased them both. It was small, only five rooms, and it was located in the centre of a large piece of ground with lawn and flowers all around. Actually, it was a somewhat old little house with a creaking set of front steps and a wonderful porch running all along the front of it where people could sit, partially screened by flowering, scented shrubs, and looked down over the big yard towards a drowsy, tree-lined avenue.

They hadn't actually meant to do more than look, but when Andrew turned to ask if Martha liked it, she was standing upon the porch in fragrant shadows looking so happy in a calm way he impulsively said, "We'll take it. But only on a lease."

She almost laughed at that last sentence. He'd learned from bitter experience about moving onto someone else's land without a lease. She remonstrated on the drive back to the agent's office.

"But we won't need it until next month, Andy, and that'll be wasting money."

"Not very much," he told her, and reached for her hand as they drove along. "You fell in love with it."

She couldn't deny that. She almost had to pinch herself to believe they'd live in it; that they'd be married people in their own home. She suddenly thought of something and gave a little start: She'd promised to see that his father was the first to know about the wedding.

"Andy . . . ?"

"Yes?"

"When — should we see the minister?"

"Did you find out about the permit and health examinations?"

She had. The permit would cost five dollars

and required both their signatures. The examination actually amounted to a pin-prick of one finger and analysis of their blood. She fidgeted. Her intention had been to wait, and while four weeks wasn't really very long in one way, in another way it was indeed very long. Because she was fundamentally honest she said, "But no one's even bought any of the wood yet. Suppose — "

"Suppose," he interrupted, "you let me worry about that."

She looked up quickly to see whether he was angry or not. He wasn't. She thought of the little house, of being there all the time with him. Of cooking and. . . .

"Andy! We don't even own a stove!"

He squeezed her fingers as he very calmly said, "We've got all afternoon to find one."

She wanted to cry. She had visions of all his remaining money going into household appliances. When the realtor pulled in up ahead, Andy had to use both hands on the steering wheel to follow the man's example. Then, she almost did cry.

After they'd signed the lease, had paid the first month's rent and were back out in the car she looked tearfully upwards. She started to say something but he bent swiftly to kiss her.

"Don't worry so much," he said. "We don't have to do it all today. Just the stove, a bed, some linens. Tomorrow. . . ."

She tried hard to be happy. It wasn't entirely a

successful undertaking but as they drove away from the realtor's office she managed to lift her spirits barely enough to snuggle close to him on the car-seat.

Buying the stove, the bed, some linens and even a breakfast-set wasn't difficult. They didn't even cost as much as she'd anticipated, although they cost enough to make her look worriedly at Andy. As a bonus the store owner gave them a handsome electric fry-pan, a large coffee pot, and of course then they had to buy a set of eating utensils and a dinner-table set of china.

After that they left the store, both of them looking a little numb. Andy said they had plenty of money left, but he acted less carefree than before too, so they didn't go look at any additional furniture that day.

In fact, when he drove her home with the rain beginning to diminish, he said he thought he'd better get right back uptown and see about selling some of their wood. Just before she left him she said they should both go see his father that night. He demurred on the grounds they wouldn't have time, and left her to go back into Carleton. She had to smile at the grim expression on his face as he drove away. He seemed to have it in mind that if he bought from local merchants they should reciprocate.

Mike was making dinner when she walked in. He cast her a quizzical glance. She walked over, threw both arms around him and kissed him, hard. Mike turned completely around to disentangle himself. He didn't have to ask, the open secret was plain to see in her misty eyes.

"You went and got married," he accused.

"No. But we rented a house and bought our first furniture."

"Andy must've sold some wood," her father said, sending her spirits plummeting again.

"No. But he's gone back into town right now to see if he can sell some because we spent an awful lot of money today, Dad."

Mike nodded, watching her closely. "I've never said yes or not, Marty. I've never butted in. Only now I want you to go somewhere and think real hard; think of all the good things and all the bad things, then total them up. Because after you've moved out of here and are his wife, it'll be too late to change your mind."

It was, she thought, sound enough advice, but it was coming almost a whole year too late. She'd already done all that adding and subtracting. But she went to her room to hang up her coat, and afterwards lay back on the bed watching rain drip dolorously down a small window.

She didn't really know exactly how she felt. Apprehensive, frightened, ecstatic, so thrilled she could scarcely breathe, so uncertain her knees were weak.

It wasn't a question of having doubts; she'd had them off and on for a year but she'd always known she'd loved Andy, wanted him more than anything else in life, so the doubts always dissolved.

It wasn't even a question of fear; she'd been afraid at night alone in her bed with all the apprehensions crowding round, and she'd been fearful when she'd been with him, but she'd overcome all that by applying herself to learning the things a Weatherby woman would be expected to know.

It was a question of her worthiness that nagged; could she measure up to what Andy and his father would expect of her; would she be able to master those amenities which meant so much up in their world?

Rachel Moody would help, she knew that, but if Lynne Weatherby hired some woman from the city, or even some of the snobbish women from Carleton who'd worked at other large estates, they'd make a point of seeing that Mike O'Toole's daughter never forgot who she was, who her father was, and where she'd come from.

She thought of their rented house, of the things they'd bought to go into it today, and her strange mood deepened. She went and washed her face in cold water telling herself this was the terrible moment every bride had to face, when all the crushing misgivings came to bow her down. She forced herself to think exclusively of the little house, which brought a smile. She'd loved it. The fact that Andy had seen that, somehow, and had rented it because of her feeling for it, made her appreciate his warmth still more.

"Supper's on!"

Mike's unexpected yell gave her a start. She examined her face in the mirror, brushed her hair a little and smoothed her dress. Then she went through the kitchen where he'd set the table, had poured them both cups of black, steaming coffee although he knew she didn't care much for coffee, and looked quizzically at her as she entered the little room.

"Not as fancy as up at the hotel dining-room," he said, making an effort to be gay, "but it don't cost near as much neither."

Actually, her father was a good cook. A surprisingly good cook. But he'd had many years to learn. He made an effort at small conversation while she weakened her coffee considerably with tinned milk. Unfortunately he wasn't as good a conversationalist as he was a cook.

But she also made an effort. They discussed many things before he finally got round to asking if she'd done that adding and subtracting he'd suggested. She said she had; that in fact she'd done the evaluating many months ago, and her sum total was perhaps even more in favour of marriage now than it had been earlier.

He didn't argue with her. He seemed to have enough insight to realize her mind was fully made up, and to also have a feeling that she had reached that mysterious period in her life when she was ripe.

Not all fathers understood how that was. Mothers knew, but the daughters themselves didn't even understand it. Nonetheless there was a particular time in every girl's life when she was at full bloom. For some it came early, even as early as age fourteen. Ordinarily though it came between seventeen and eighteen. Martha was one of those girls who had blossomed late. Beautifully, symmetrically, voluptuously, but late.

Her father said if there was nothing more to discuss, if they already had the house rented, their minds made up, their plans crystallized, then only one thing was left for them to do — get married quickly.

She finished the coffee, played with her food a while longer then stopped even pretending to be hungry. "Tomorrow," she said. "Perhaps the day after tomorrow."

He smiled. "Sure, Marty," and seemed to also lose his appetite. He arose, made a gesture at the table saying dishes could wait and jerked his head at her. It was no longer raining out. In fact it had quit while she'd been in her room.

"Come on; let's go down by the creek and take advantage of the coolness."

For once her conscience didn't wince as she walked away leaving the kitchen looking as it did.

Outside, the sky was scrubbed clean, every star was highly polished and the thickening moon was finally beginning to cast a little light of its own. There were bats overhead and frogs down in the warm mud of the creek-bank. Fireflies winked on and off as they floated just above the water and mosquitoes came at once, but they had Mike's aerosol can of repellent to take care of that.

He'd given the boat another coat of leaded paint. It dully shone. He leaned on it as he turned and said, "You know, honey, when I rode up there looking for Andy with Mister Weatherby in the Land Rover he talked a little to me'n the chauffeur. He said he thought Andy'd picked the best girl for him, anywhere around. If he hadn't said that I'd have been worried about you marryin' into the Weatherbys." Mike smiled at her in the weak light. "You'll show 'em. Maybe an O'Toole isn't a Weatherby, but we got our share o' pride and grit too."

Chapter Eighteen

Andrew came by but only for a brief visit before going on. He said he'd got a room in town for the night because after all that rain the old abandoned county road would be too muddy for auto use. He told her he'd managed to sell — and collect for — three cords of wood. He even showed her the cheque. It made her spirits rise. The fact that he was so pleased helped. They hadn't got back as much as they'd spent but they'd got back a respectable part of it.

Also, he told her he had leads where he might be able to sell more wood. He left the cheque with her with instructions to go put it into his account the following day because he'd be heading up into the woods in the morning before the bank opened. He kissed her and departed.

They hadn't discussed the house or their wedding plans but standing there in the kitchen looking at the cheque she was only conscious that this slip of paper was her first responsibility to their union as well as the first money he'd earned as a married man — well, as practically a married man. She smiled and went off to bed.

The following morning they were at breakfast, she and her father, when they heard the car drive in out back. Neither had any idea who it might be coming this early until Andy barged in looking stricken as well as darkly angry.

"The road's closed," he blurted out. "There's a big logging chain across it from one tree to another tree."

Martha sat and stared but her father wrinkled his brow. "Closed? How can that be; that road, such as it is, has been open ever since I can remember."

"It's not open now, Mister O'Toole. There's a 'No Trespassing' sign nailed to one of the trees right above that big chain. Whoever put the chain there picked the best spot; the trees are so thick up there I couldn't even find a way to drive around it."

Martha said, "Andy; does that mean you can't get up where the wood is stacked?"

"It also means I can't even get on past to where I'm cutting now."

Mike got up. "Sit down," he mumbled. "I'll get you some coffee."

As her father moved towards the pot on the stove Martha thought of the cheque. Her heart sank. "Were you supposed to deliver that wood you sold last night?" she asked.

He shook his head. "No; they'll come after it. I quoted three dollars more a cord for loading and

hauling and they said they'd come after it themselves."

"But they can't go after it, Andy."

"That's right," he agreed, then looked up as
Mike brought his coffee. "Mister O'Toole; hasn't
that always been a county road?"

Mike returned to his chair, sat down and
screwed up his face as though to expound, then
he suddenly snapped his lips closed, looked at
them both a moment and finally said, "Well, yes;
Andy. Only I recall reading in the legal notices of
the newspaper six, seven years back where the
County give notice of abandonment 'cause the
road didn't go anywhere and because it cost too
much to maintain a road no one lived on."

Andy groaned, reached for his coffee, sipped it
black then leaned back in the chair he'd taken at
the table. "Damn," he exclaimed. "If that's right
Jamison may be able to make it stick; may be able
to close the road." He reached, gulped down the
last of the coffee, jumped up and said he'd be
back later then rushed out of the house.

Martha said nothing until the sound of his car
faded. "Mister Jamison wouldn't do a thing like
that unless he was sure of himself."

Mike shrugged. All he knew of Jamison was
what he'd seen out front of the hotel. That was
enough to incline him towards some harsh
thoughts. He picked up the fork he'd dropped
when Andy'd come busting in and resumed
breakfast.

"It's spite, Dad. Jamison defied Mister

Weatherby in town and now he's doing this out of spite."

"Maybe, Marty. But I wouldn't want to be in Jamison's boots if that's so. Mister Weatherby could be a Tartar if you got him roiled up."

Martha couldn't eat any more. She began clearing the table. They didn't have a telephone but she briefly thought of calling Rachel Moody. Not that Rachel would be able to do anything but right then Martha needed someone to talk to.

Mike had to go upriver to the salt-water where the Pawtucket met the sound and set his lobster traps. He'd borrowed a boat for this purpose. He also intended to hasten straight back and finish leading, caulking and painting his own craft so that the following morning when he'd go see what he'd caught he'd be able to use his own boat again. It was a rather tight schedule so he left right after breakfast after admonishing Martha not to worry. An inane bit of advice but springing from the best intentions in the world.

She thought about going to see Lynne Weatherby, about going in search of John Richards — anyone at all she could talk to. In the end she found an excuse to drive up into town — they needed baking powder, flour and sugar. There, she met Charley Prentiss, the constable. They'd grown up together. Charley was from shantytown too, originally, although now he didn't even go back down there unless it was in the performance of his duty. She blurted out to

179

Charley what had happened. He was a burly man, young and tough but pleasant enough if given the chance to be pleasant.

Of course he knew about Andy Weatherby striking out on his own. He also knew all the gossip about Andy and Martha, and where most folks disapproved he approved most heartily. Having come from a similar environment he was grimly pleased that Martha was going to get away from the creek too.

He listened, then said, "I don't know this Jamison, Marty, but I know one thing — he can't close that road."

"Dad says it was abandoned, Charley."

"Don't matter, he can't close it. I been reading law three years so I know for a fact that if anyone lives above you on a road you got to let them have access."

"Charley. No one lives above the old hotel."

"They own land up there, Marty. That feller over in Jersey who owns the land Andy's cuttin' on now has a right to access. So has everyone else who owns land above the old hotel. This Jamison can't just arbitrarily close off the road."

"Andy said he'd put a logging chain across it and put up 'No Trespassing' signs."

Prentiss's coarse, resolute features clouded. "All right," he said, "you forget about it. I'll go call the County Attorney at the Court House and see about this."

She didn't forget about it. She couldn't have if she'd wanted to. But Charley Prentiss had given her fresh hope, so she went on, did her shopping and was climbing back into the old car when she saw Jamison across the road out front of the hotel smoking a cigar.

She considered going over there, but she didn't know what she'd say, so when his gaze drifted around, saw her and settled upon her in the car, she punched the starter and drove off without looking back.

It was a humid, sticky day. Steam rose from the earth after the rain, and the sun was riding across a cloudless sky. By the time she got back home her father had returned and was down working on his boat. After she'd put the groceries away she went down there.

He asked where she'd been. After she told him she also related what the town constable had said. Mike turned that over in his mind and nodded. It made sense, he told her. Then he said, "You know, I got to thinking while I was laying the traps, Marty. Keep an eye on Andy. I've got a feeling that if he runs into Mister Jamison he might do something he'd be sorry for later on."

She wasn't sure, after a moment of reflection, that she'd be the least bit regretful for whatever Andy might do to Jamison but she didn't say that because someone hooted a soft greeting from up by the house.

It was John Richards. He came striding down where Martha and Mike waited. She told him what had happened and his little blue eyes puckered up until they were hidden by dark pouches of leathery hide. Old John had nothing to say right away; instead he looked round, found the rotting stump and eased down upon it. She also told him what the town constable had said and old John nodded thoughtfully, still without comment.

After a bit he said, "Well; seems whenever I got good news some else's done come along first with bad news." He quietly smiled at her. "Miz' Moody agreed to go back to work for Mist' Weatherby. Thought you'd want to know 'cause she said she'd never step foot inside that house again until he agreed to face up to the facts of life about you'n Andy."

Mike said, "Does that mean he's on their side, Mister Richards?"

"Sure seems that way, Mist' O'Toole. But I haven't talked to her since yesterday morning and only talked to him long enough to be told she'd agreed to come back, before he went bustin' it down to the city."

"He's not around?" asked Mike, his thoughts transparent.

"No," averred old John. "But don't fret about that. He'll be back this evening some time. And I wouldn't want to be in Mister Jamison's boots when he does get back."

John considered Martha's stricken expression and smiled at her, his earlier shock no longer visible. "Don't you fret, young lady. Jamison'll be lucky if someone don't use his log-chain to hang him by."

Martha was feeling more encouraged as the day wore on. John Richards was one of those individuals who took most things in stride; he had a way of acting cheerful even when he didn't feel very cheerful. But what he'd said coupled to what Charley Prentiss had told her, made the gloom dissolve. She said she'd go put the coffee pot on and left them beside the boat.

Mike studied old John a while then said, "I never saw two kids with such a knack for gettin' upset before in all my life, Mister Richards."

John gave his head a slight toss. "You been a married man, Mist' O'Toole; you know it's not any bed of roses despite what the motion pictures and magazines say. As for those two — I wouldn't fret too much. Andy's set on being independent, which is just right, but it don't hurt none havin' folks like you'n me — and his pappy — standing back watching over them a little. By the way; how's the lobster business?"

"Slow," said Mike, turning back to finish painting his boat. "I got to thinking today whilst I was up near the sound where you can hear the sea crashing along the coves: A good row-boat lasts just about as long as a man. Now this boat's got the rot. I fixed it this time, so it'll last another few years, but it was a sign, Mist' Richards. It's not a young boat any longer and I'm not a young man." Mike paused to look and see whether John was listening. He was. Sunshine beat hotly down into the damp place where they were but John sat perched on the old stump as though heat were the least of his troubles.

"And now my girl'll leave me," went on Mike. "Did you ever have any children?"

John shook his head.

"But you're a feeling man," said Mike, insistently. "You can guess about what it'll be like alone down here with just the shack, the boat, the lobster traps."

Finally old John stood up. "You sure take a long while to get up to what you're thinking," he said bluntly, but with a soft smile. "What's on your mind?"

"I was wondering. . . . You suppose Mister Weatherby'd need another gardener up there at the estate?"

John's smile lingered but his eyes puckered shrewdly. "'You know anything about gardening?" he asked.

"No. But then I've heard tell you didn't know much more when he hired you, Mister Richards."

That was true of course. But John looked like a man who'd just seen an abyss at his feet. He said, "That'd have to be between you'n Mister Weatherby."

"But you could put in a good word."

"I reckon," drawled old John, and looked up towards the house where Martha was waving for them to come on over. "It'd be a mite awkward," he said to Mike while still gazing up at Martha. "Take a lot of tact. You figure you could handle it, Mist' O'Toole? I've seen enough Yankees these last three, four years to know they aren't real strong on tact."

Mike straightened up, wiped his hands on his trousers and softly smiled at old John. "Are Texans?" he asked.

John chuckled. "Come along; let's have some of that coffee. All right; if I get the chance I'll put in a good word for you. But Mister O'Toole if you're put to working with me, the first time you show up drunk I'm goin' to set you out in the sun and maybe stake you out over an anthill."

They started up towards the house side by side, both of them looking a little pleased about something.

Chapter Nineteen

Andy returned in mid-afternoon. He'd been to see the attorney, he told Martha, Mike and John, who had drawn up that Agreement with the man over in Jersey. That barrister has told him he didn't see how Jamison could possibly close the old road without first bringing suit in court to show intent. But he'd also sent Andy over to see the County Attorney.

There, Andy said, he discovered that someone else was irate over the road too. Charley Prentiss the town constable had called while Andy was in the County Attorney's office. The County Attorney had told Charley he'd call him back. He also told Andy he'd have to search the files to make certain no one had officially brought a suit to quiet-title on the old road before issuing an order for the log-chain to be removed. Andy said the County Attorney acted a little wary, particularly after Prentiss's call. However, he did tell them that the attorney had said, if that old road hadn't legally reverted to the landowners over whose property it passed, then Jamison nor any-one else could close it.

"As for landowners above the old hotel," he concluded, "the attorney said if any of them wished to bring suit against Jamison they could probably force him to cease and desist."

Old John, listening in deep silence through all this, drawled an opinion of his own. "In my day, Andy, when someone got on a high horse and did something like that . . . we rode out an' had a little hand-to-hand talk with him. Mind now, I'm not advocatin' violence. I'm a right peaceable man." John smiled. "When a feller gets my age he's got to be peaceable. All I'm saying is that this 'cease and desist' kind o' talk is likely to make things drag on until the rains come, then you won't be able to cut any more wood until next summer. And that could hurt you a mite."

Andy snorted. "Hurt me a *lot.*"

Martha thought she heard something and crossed to a window. A dark, shiny sedan was creeping cautiously down through the thicket on their little road. She couldn't see the driver and didn't recognize the car so she called to the others that a stranger was arriving.

It turned out not to be exactly a stranger. It was Constable Prentiss. When he entered the house the only one he didn't know was John Richards. Andy took care of that and Martha went to get another cup and saucer for Charley Prentiss's coffee. He hung his hat on the back of a chair, thanked Martha for the coffee and said to Andy, "I got two wrecking bars, a hacksaw and a propane torch." He didn't elaborate. He sipped coffee waiting for them to understand what all those destructive tools were for.

" 'County Attorney called you back?" asked Andy. "I was sitting in his office when you called this morning."

Prentiss set aside the empty cup. "Yeah, he called me back. Whoever put that chain up has no right to close the road. At least not like that. If he wants to try through court and advertise his intentions in the paper as is required by law, maybe he could close it, but not with no chain."

Mike rubbed his palms together. He was beginning to enjoy this. "You're going up there to cut the chain, Charley?"

"Yep. Cut it, hack it, or torch the lock. Then I got to go find this Jamison and give him notice what I done and that if he puts up another chain he'll be in breach o' the law and subject to arrest."

Andy arose. "I'll go with you," he said.

Prentiss nodded solemnly. Martha started to speak but old John put a hand over her arm and silenced her. He was shrewdly watching the two burly younger men. "You'll be right careful," he said. "I don't know anything about this Jamison but I know enough about folks in general to figure he's not goin' to like what you're doing if he happens to be up there."

"He's back in town," said Prentiss, reaching for his hat as Andy crossed to the door. "I saw him eatin' in the hotel dining-room. 'Made a point to see him before I left town. Let's go, Andy."

Old John didn't take his hand off Martha's arm until the door had closed, then he said, "Just give 'em a few minutes." He looked quietly at Mike. "That old car of your'n able to make it up that old road, Mister O'Toole?"

"That old car of mine," said Mike a little testily, "can go on any road in the county — Mister Richards!"

John laughed, went over to the stove to calmly re-fill his cup, returned with the pot and re-filled Mike's cup as well, then put the pot aside and looked at Martha.

"Nothing's going to happen," he said. "Why; cutting a chain's about as dangerous as fallin' asleep after supper. But we'll ride up there directly and sort of see how things are going. I figure Andy'll drive on through to where he's sawing now, and I also figure that lawman'll head straight back to town. *That's* the only time when Jamison could come along and mess things up. We'll sort of park up there and see that he don't. That's all."

"I've got a shotgun," said Mike.

Martha looked aghast. John shook his head while he sipped coffee. "No weapons," he stated. "Folks don't get hurt much without weapons, but they sure do when they *got* weapons."

Martha's stomach was knotted. She'd never had anything to do with the law before, therefore she was fearful when it intruded into her life. Her father's remark about a gun heightened her dread too. It was John Richards' great depth of calm that kept her from crying out against every-thing that was happening. She began to lean more and more upon old John. She could have done a whole lot worse.

They left the house fifteen minutes later. As John said when they were in the old car, it would be better if they didn't arrive up there until after the chain had been removed and both Prentiss and young Weatherby had gone on a mile or so to where Andy had his new camp.

Mike knew the old road very well. They had to go westerly along the interstate highway a mile or more before cutting back across the creek where another road showed up, and where several shantytown homes squatted. The bridge wasn't very good; strong enough, but weathered. Beyond that they had fresh tracks to follow the full distance. Rain had made the dirt road muddy in the low places but otherwise it was tractable enough.

Mike stopped once, a half mile or so above the bridge where another shack clung to a mud-bank beside the road. That was the home of the man he'd borrowed the row-boat from the day before. He waved and a loafing individual upon a littered porch waved back. But that hadn't been Mike's reason for stopping; he leaned out to listen. He said there wasn't a sound, eased the car into low range and crept on again.

Martha asked what would happen if Jamison

caught them beyond the 'No Trespassing' sign. Mike said he believed that as long as Jamison didn't own the roadway, and as long as they didn't get off it onto Jamison's land, he didn't believe there was anything the city-man could do.

John was more reassuring. As it turned out he was also very wrong, but at the time he didn't think so. He said, "Pshaw, girl; what'd a feller like Jamison be doing up here this late in the day anyway? Quit your worrying, we won't see him."

They eased around through the dark underbrush with very little afternoon sky showing through matted tree limbs overhead, and saw the sign forbidding anyone to trespass beyond that point. There was no chain in sight until they got right up between the two huge trees where the sign hung, then old John pointed into the weeds on the right side. Someone had meticulously coiled the chain at the base of a tree as though it had been a rattlesnake. Mike grunted about that.

"Charley did that. I know his sense of humour."

They stopped there. Mike cut the engine and climbed down followed by Martha and John. It was clear what had been done. The chain itself hadn't been hurt at all but someone had used a very hot flame on the big padlock; it was twisted and discoloured where it had been neatly placed in the very centre of the coils of chain.

They listened but detected no sound on ahead. Martha peered apprehensively about. It was a gloomy, dark and forbidding place. If old John and her father hadn't been right there she'd have fled.

John went over beside the chain and sat down. "Might as well get comfortable," he said. "Andy'll be up there for a spell."

"Why here?" she asked. "Why not go on up where they are, Mister Richards?"

John jutted his jaw back the way they'd come. "Just sort of set and wait," he drawled. "I don't expect Jamison'll show up at all — not one chance in a hundred, the way I see it — but all the same if he *did* come up, an' if he set this cussed chain again — how would Andy and the lawman drive back out?"

Mike nodded. "It would be a long walk," he agreed, and moved over to sit on a stump beside John.

Martha walked on up the road a short distance hoping to either hear Andy and Charley Prentiss or perhaps catch sight of them. She did neither and returned to the gloomy spot where her father and John were idly talking.

Off to their right were several of the neat, long racks of cordwood. Mike and John were interested in them. Neither of them had ever operated a chain saw so they were very impressed by the neat cuts and the amount of wood which had been bucked up. John tried to guess, at current rates, how much money all that wood represented. Mike thought it had to be somewhere in the neighbourhood of seven or eight hundred dollars worth.

Martha listened to them and got calm again. They acted as though there was nothing at all to do but just sit and wait, which in fact it seemed was all they actually had to do. Then she heard the auto coming.

She spun to look back down the dingy, dark roadway. The car was distant yet but its sound was unmistakably approaching. She turned. John and Mike were sitting like a pair of stone images looking in the same direction. They had also heard it. Old John picked up a stone, heaved it away and said, "Well; looks like my one chance in a hundred's about to drive up here." He stood up.

"Wish I'd brought the shotgun," said Mike.

John snorted. "Your car's the best weapon you could have right now. It's settin' in the middle of the road. If that's Jamison coming he's not goin' nowhere except back the way he came. He can't pass and since he picked this spot he'll know it."

Martha's heart was beating unevenly. She tried to convince herself they were doing nothing wrong, which in fact they weren't, but that didn't keep her from being very apprehensive. She'd seen Jamison angry once before when he'd faced Lynne Weatherby. She knew he could be difficult. She also knew neither her father nor old John Richards would be a match for him if he became violent. She wished she were up the road a mile where Andy and Charley were.

"I can run up and get Charley," she said

swiftly, with the sound of the approaching car louder.

"No need," insisted old John, calm as always, his small eyes puckered, his brawny old raw-boned hands hanging loosely at his side. "Anyway he'll be here and have had his say before they could get back down here." He looked at Mike, then over at Martha. "Now don't go getting all upset, Missy. We got a right to be where we are." The shrewd blue eyes drifted back to Mike. "You got the keys out of your car, Mister O'Toole?"

Mike nodded swiftly, watching the road like a hawk.

"He'll ask you to move it — if it's Jamison. Don't do it. We'll just sort of argue and fumble round until Andy and the constable come drivin' back down here. That shouldn't be very hard, should it?"

Neither of them answered him. They caught their first sight of the car. None of them recognized it but then they wouldn't have anyway since they'd never seen Jamison's automobile before.

But they recognized the man behind the wheel as soon as he rounded the curve and saw them standing there beside the road with Mike's old jalopy blocking the right-of-way.

" 'Be switched," muttered John. "A hundred to one and I sure-'nough lost. It's him all right."

Jamison stopped, sat a moment glaring through his windscreen, then cut his engine, flung open the door and sprang out. He'd seen the coiled chain at the base of the big tree. He didn't say a word but strode on over and stood staring at the mangled padlock. When he slowly lifted his eyes Martha saw the rusty colour coming into his face. She involuntarily put a hand to her lips. Her father recoiled from the expression of raw violence too but old John stood as relaxed and easy as ever.

Chapter Twenty

Jamison said in a reedy tone, "Which one of you destroyed my lock and removed that chain?"

John was blunt. "Why?"

"Because I'm going to make a citizen's arrest right here and take him back to Carleton to be booked into jail — that's why. Was it you, old man?"

John was slow answering. He looked over at Martha then round at her father. Finally he shook his head in Jamison's direction. "Nope. It wasn't me, feller. And it wasn't Mister O'Toole either." John smiled. "Of course it wasn't Miss O'Toole."

Jamison kept stonily gazing at the three of them. "Weatherby," he said, letting his glance drift to the roadway where tracks showed plainly upon soft dirt. "He's still up there. Just one set of tracks means he hasn't come back yet." He looked back at old John. "Well . . . ?"

"Believe what you like, mister, but before it gets you into a heap of trouble I'd like to pass you a little advice."

"Shut up!" Jamison looked at Martha again. "I know who you are now, young lady, and I can guess about this other man. I've been asking some questions since Weatherby tried to bluff me in the roadway. I think I have a fairly accurate picture of where all of you fit into this mess. Maybe you'd like to know I could have the lot of you jailed for what you've done here today. How do you suppose old Weatherby would like that?"

"Not very well," said John frankly. "I'm his gardener on the estate. This here is his son's wife-to-be. That's her pappy. And of course if you wait a spell you might get his son too. Naw; I don't reckon Mister Weatherby'd like it a-tall." John chuckled at some private thought. "But Mister Jamison, I got a feeling you'd regret tryin' to get us locked up a heap more'n Mister Weatherby'd dislike getting us out again."

"Weatherby," spat Jamison, "doesn't scare me in the least. I take no orders from him. In case you're interested, the company I work for is operated independently of the York and Westchester Bank and Trust Company. I called down and reported what happened up here. My orders were to use my own discretion." Jamison gazed at the ruined lock, at the neatly coiled chain at his feet. "I think I'll do exactly that. I'll teach Weatherby to try and embarrass me on the sidewalk in front of others. I'll rub his damned nose in it before I'm through."

Martha moved over a little closer. "Mister Jamison; the County Attorney authorized the removal of your chain. He said you'd have to sue in court to officially close this road."

Jamison's eyes dropped to the chain then lifted to Martha's face. "Did he say that gave you people the right to destroy my property?"

"We'll buy you another lock," said Martha, trying to placate Jamison. She took one more step forward and faced him. In a very soft tone she said, "This isn't at all necessary, Mister Jamison. You can understand why Mister Weatherby was upset the other day. You can also understand our interest. You're an intelligent person. Wouldn't it be a lot easier if we tried to start over? Andy won't cut any more wood off your land. That was what you wanted stopped wasn't it?"

Jamison did, in fact, calm down a little, but instead of showing rusty high colour, he now showed vindictive hatred in his narrowed eyes. "All right, Miss O'Toole," he softly said. "We'll start over. I won't press charges over the destruction of my property."

Martha knew from the cold fire in his eyes this was only the beginning of whatever he had to say, nevertheless she said, "Thank you."

"But," snapped Jamison, "I'll give young Weatherby exactly twenty-four hours to remove his wood from my land!"

Obviously, that was impossible. There were too many cords of wood to be moved even if John and Mike and Martha helped move it. Those racked up tiers and cords stretched for hundreds of feet. The only way anyone could move all that cordwood would be if they hired a gang of about ten men and worked them round the clock the full twenty-four hours.

Old John's little eyes drew out narrow, his mouth flattened over his teeth. He looked dangerous. Martha saw that even as she realized how Jamison had taken advantage of her appeal for peace to make his impossible demand. But she didn't want old John to do anything rash. He was no match for Jamison; he was no longer a young man.

Jamison had also seen the transformation in Richards. His cold smile came up again. He looked at Martha as though he were hoping John would do something violent. He was a strong, tough-looking person despite his city pallor.

She said, "You know that's impossible, Mister Jamison. I'm trying to avert trouble. You're trying to force it."

"That's right," snapped Jamison, still watching old John, his voice as soft as silk. "You people and Weatherby think you can walk over me. I'm going to teach the lot of you some manners." He paused, waiting for John to make up his mind whether to act or not. John acted, but in a way that surprised Martha and her father.

"Mike," he said, "back your car around so's Mister Jamison can drive on past."

Mike looked surprised. He blinked several times, then turned to wordlessly obey. Martha was also surprised, but she thought she knew why John had given that order. She turned on her heel to go with her father.

John said, "All right, mister; you're pretty well callin' the tune right now. So you maybe win this go-round. We'll let you pass."

Jamison laughed, loosened where he stood and turned to watch the O'Tooles climb into their old car. "I didn't expect any sense from you," he said, showing contempt, "but maybe you're smarter than I figured, old-timer."

It took a lot of jockeying for Mike to get his car backed clear but he worked at it and eventually was clear enough so that Jamison could squeeze by. Then he cut the engine, slumped over the steering wheel and looked over where Jamison and Richards still stood.

The sun was nearly gone but in among the tall trees and rank underbrush there wasn't much change; the light failed slightly but since it had never been very bright anyway none of the people noticed.

Jamison got into his car, gunned the engine once then drove past O'Toole, slowed as though to halt for his chain, then seemed to change his mind and kept on driving. John waited until he'd disappeared around a yonder curve then ran to the car, climbed in and said, "Get going, Mister O'Toole. Herd him right on up the road and we'll block him from backing off."

Martha had already explained to her father this was what she'd thought old John had in mind: Herding Jamison up where he thought he'd encounter only Andrew Weatherby.

Mike was sweating hard but he obeyed, clutching the wheel in nervous hands. By the time they got around the first curve Jamison was out of sight around the next one. They drove a little faster and came upon him a half mile ahead. He'd stopped.

"Heard us trailing' him," said old John, and craned ahead. "Where'n hell's that lawman?"

"There," panted Mike, pointing with one hand up where two thick-set youths suddenly appeared out of the brush in the centre of the yonder roadway. "Thank the Lord!"

But Jamison hadn't seen anyone else; he was out of his car now, angrily striding back to intercept Mike's car. John told Mike to stop. They all piled out quickly, before Jamison could reach them. As John said afterwards, he had no wish to be caught sitting inside a car when someone was mad enough to take a swing at him.

Jamison swore fiercely at them as he approached, hands balled into fists, shoulders hunched forward. Behind him a little distance beyond where his car stood, Andy and Charley Prentiss started moving. They'd evidently heard the cursing. Martha was frightened. She'd heard men curse before, that was no novelty, but she'd never before had a cursing man bearing down on her with his fisted hands coming up or with wrath distorting his face like this. She winced a little, moving closer to her father.

Mike was no fighting man, that was clear enough, but evidently neither was he a coward for he stepped sideways in front of his daughter and closer to John Richards.

It was old John who broke the spell and interrupted Jamison's snarls. He stooped, picked up a heavy stick from the ground and took two steps forward to meet Jamison. At once the younger man halted.

That was when Charley Prentiss, passing quickly around Jamison's car up the road, called out.

"Mister; you back off and shut your mouth!"

Jamison whirled, astonishment on his face as he saw, not just Andrew Weatherby, but the burly figure with the gun and badge.

Charley came straight on, halted a few feet from Jamison, told old John to drop the club, which John did, then Charley turned his angry gaze upon the city-man.

"You got a big mouth," he said. "Get over there beside your car, face it and place both hands atop it."

Jamison made his first big mistake. He said, "Listen here, Constable. . . ." Andrew grabbed him, spun him half around, caught his belt and hurled him against the car. Martha was rooted where she stood. So was her father, but old John was grinning from ear to ear.

Charley moved swiftly to keep Andy from reaching Jamison again. He said, "Both hands atop the car!"

Jamison recovered his balance, glared, then slowly turned to obey. Charley roughly ran his hands up and down Jamison's body, then swung him by the shoulder so they were facing one another again. Charley looked as though he hoped Jamison would resist. Martha, who remembered Charley's brawling reputation in school, hoped Jamison wouldn't make another mistake.

"In case you didn't know," said Charley, "I'm the one who burnt off your lock and took down that chain, Mister Jamison. By order of the County Attorney. This is not a private thoroughfare. If you want to make it one you'll have to get an attorney, advertise your intention in the local paper, then try and prove no one needs access above the hotel site."

Jamison said, "These people. . . ." and let it dwindle off as he looked from face to face. Every eye that was on him was hostile.

"Yes?" said Andy. "What about these people?"

But Jamison didn't try to complete his accusation. He ignored Andy too and said to Constable Prentiss, "I'll get an attorney. You can bet on it, Constable. And for your brutality I'll sue the city of Carleton, too."

Charley was unperturbed. "Go ahead and have at it," he growled, then pointed. "Get in your car, back it off the road and go on back to town. Don't get cute, Mister Jamison, because I'll be right behind you every inch of the way."

Jamison's eyes widened. "Why should I go back with you?" he demanded.

"Because you're under arrest."

"I'm — *what?* I've done nothing at all. Furthermore this land — "

"This land," interrupted Prentiss, "happens to be a county road. You're not on private property. And you're under arrest for resisting an officer of the law, for molesting these people on a public right-of-way, and for using abusive language. Now turn that car around and get back down the road!"

Jamison looked stunned. He and Charley Prentiss exchanged a long, steady stare before Jamison finally pulled himself together and climbed into his car. Charley turned towards Mike O'Toole. "Back off so we can go by, Mike." His last order was to Andrew. "You ride back to the O'Toole place with Mike, Andy. I'll have to stay with Jamison all the way into town. All right?"

Andy nodded. It was fine with him. He'd stepped over beside Martha and was holding her hand. For the first time in several hours she dared relax. Andy led her over to the side of the dark and gloomy old road while Jamison jockeyed his car back and forth to get it turned. Charley Prentiss jogged back up after his sedan, which was already facing in the correct direction, so by the time Jamison got turned Charley was already coming in behind him.

As Jamison started past where Martha, Andy and old John stood, he poked his head out the window. Andy immediately let go of Martha's hand and took a forward step. Whatever Jamison had meant to say, he didn't try and get out, but his glare was murderous as he eased out the clutch and started back the way he'd come.

Charley Prentiss went past with a grave nod at them, unsmiling and tough-eyed. Old John blew out a big breath, went over where Mike was and said he'd walk ahead to find a place where Mike could reverse his auto.

Martha watched her father move the car out then turned and leaned upon Andy. "He was furious," she murmured. "I thought he was going to attack us, Andy."

"That would have been a sad day for him," exclaimed young Weatherby, and kissed her on the forehead.

"But now he'll make serious trouble for us, Andy."

"He's already done that, love. He can't make it any worse no matter what he does."

Chapter Twenty-One

Charley Prentiss came by the following morning to talk to Martha. Jamison had been released on bond and had got an attorney in town. Charley said he was fighting mad; that he'd said, while they'd been booking him into jail the evening before, he'd make them all wish they'd never been born before he was finished with them.

Martha thought Charley was troubled but not afraid. He said he was going on up and talk to Andy where he was cutting wood. He asked if she'd like to ride along. She almost agreed, then thought better of it. John Richards had said Mister Weatherby would return from the city last night; she told Charley she had a few errands of her own to run and went out to the car with him.

"Can he really make that much trouble?" she asked.

Prentiss had been an officer of the law just long enough to know that *anyone* could make trouble if they were willing to spend enough money to do it. He said, "He's going to file a petition for re-

206

dress with the Town Council claiming police brutality. I'm not much worried about that, Marty. But he got a good attorney, so he can make trouble all right — unless someone jumps in with a better attorney."

She knew what Charley meant and nodded without comment. As he climbed in and started his engine she said, "Tell Andy to come and see me when he quits this evening, will you?"

Prentiss nodded and drove off.

Mike had taken his boat out early to check the traps up near the sound. He'd seemed anxious to get away in fact, and she could understand how he felt. Her father had never been a troublesome man. Sly, raffish, scheming, yes. Troublesome, no.

She went back to change her clothes — she'd been wearing a work blouse and dungarees. When she came forth again into the golden sunshine she was attired in a pale green dress, had her curly short hair brushed until it shone, and looked very resolute. Today the people she and Andy had bought the appliances and furniture from would be delivering them to the little house they'd rented. She'd have to see to that too. In fact, that was her first stop in town. She left orders for nothing to be delivered until afternoon when she'd be at the house to show the men where to put things.

After that, she headed straight for the Weatherby estate and oddly enough, the front wrought-iron gates were open. She hesitated, wondering whether she shouldn't telephone ahead anyway, then she saw John Richards up the drive a hundred or so yards talking with another tall man and drove right on in.

Both men turned as they heard her car. She didn't realize the other man was Lynne Weatherby himself until she was close enough to slack off. He and John started towards her.

She cut the engine and climbed down. The two older men towered above her. Mister Weatherby nodded gravely without smiling. "We were just discussing you," he said, "and other things."

"Charley Prentiss has gone up to find Andy," she told them, then related all that Prentiss had told her. As she spoke she saw the subtle change come over Mister Weatherby's lean, sun-tanned features. He looked almost sardonic.

"Don't worry about any of it," he told her, and turned as a deep gong sounded from the house. "Excuse me," he said, and moved away.

John explained. "That's the telephone. He's got a call." Then John said, "I told him what happened yesterday, Missy. He'll look into it."

She wasn't satisfied with that. "What can he do, Mister Richards? Jamison has Charley Prentiss worried, and I've known Charley all my life. He doesn't frighten easily."

John's eyes ironically twinkled. "Well; if you got some notion Mister Weatherby scares easy you got another notion coming. When he tells someone not to worry — they can quit then and there."

Martha saw a short sturdy figure in crisp white

move out onto the large verandah. "Miss Moody," she murmured.

John nodded. "Yeh. Sure is, isn't it; she came back yesterday afternoon. Now all Mister Weatherby's got to do is straighten out the trouble with Andy. He'll do it. He's not an easy man to turn aside."

Martha felt better. "I'd better go now, Mister Richards. I just wanted Mister Weatherby to know the threats Mister Jamison had made."

"Sure-'nough," he drawled. "I got an idea Mist' Weatherby'd like for you to stay until he comes back. He might have something to tell you."

Martha extricated herself though, saying Mister Weatherby must be a very busy man and she'd already taken up too much of his time. John tried harder to delay her, but she got back into the old car, said she had to be at the rented house when the furniture arrived, and departed.

All the way back through town to the little house she thought of how Lynne Weatherby's quiet, calm and poised manner calmed a person's fears. She thought it had less to do with his wealth than his personal strength; he was a man who knew what to do in any situation. She reflected a little, wondering if that's what it was that made some men successful, others failures. She couldn't imagine Lynne Weatherby being struck dumb yesterday as her father had been.

Not that she had belittling thoughts of Mike. She was simply thinking about the differences which made men as they were. Mike hadn't known what to say or do during the unpleasant confrontation with Mister Jamison. He'd have defended her and he'd have fought if Jamison had attacked old John, but he'd only have done so because he'd have been dragged into it. She thought Lynne Weatherby would have somehow seized the initiative; she had no idea how he could have done that, but she was certain he would have. She also felt that he'd have humbled Jamison too.

The little house was quiet and serene on its back street. She drove in, left Mike's old car and went up to the porch. There were dozens of birds in trees and shrubbery, some singing in the sunlight, some scolding, a few busy seeking insects impervious to any intrusion, even one by a human being.

It was very peaceful. She had no idea why some builder had placed the house so far back from the roadway, but she was glad he had. Perhaps he'd been someone who liked seeing greenery between himself and civilization.

He'd left the great trees standing, which was in itself a revelation, because most people sensibly cut down any tree that might topple someday and cave in the roof, or which might clutter the down-spouts and drains with autumn leaves.

There was a weathered picket fence down beside the paved front sidewalk but it was visible only here and there where shrubbery didn't totally conceal it.

She went inside. The little house had a musty, forlorn air. She went round opening windows to air out the rooms. The papering was old-fashioned and the kitchen floor needed shoring up from beneath; it creaked when she trod upon it.

There was a rather steep and narrow little stairway leading to a pair of dormer rooms upstairs. The only place a person as large as Andy could stand erect was in the very centre of those two little rooms. Otherwise the rafters sloped away too abruptly on both sides. She felt the heat up there and left more windows open. Those rooms, she thought, had belonged to children. The wall-paper gave her that clue.

The men arrived with their appliances and furniture. She supervised the unloading and watched as a bald, jolly man with a paunch hooked things up. He knew who she was although she didn't know him. He also knew Andy. He told her he'd installed Alice Weatherby's appliances when Andy's parents had first bought and remodelled their big fieldstone house. He said Andy looked exactly like his mother.

After the men left she stood in her kitchen wondering how they were going to make out with little more than the barest essentials. Then she smiled. As far as the world knew, they had everything they needed. She went out into the rear yard. It was only about a third the size of the front yard and had a black old cedar fence along the rear property line which was covered with morning-glories. There were several thick old rose bushes out there giving off a fragrance as sweet as anything she'd ever smelled.

But everything needed care; whoever had lived here the last few years hadn't done much maintaining. The grass was rank and had rust spots. She thought they'd have to buy a mower for the grass, several long hoses, and some chemical fertiliser. There was an awful lot that needed doing.

She strolled round front, found a crate and put it on the porch for a chair. That's where she was sitting when the sleek convertible turned the corner, cruised slowly forward and wheeled up into the driveway. Her heart gave a little skip. Andy was hatless, wearing his oily work clothes, and when he climbed out to come forward he wasn't smiling.

She slowly arose and went as far as the steps to meet him. "What's wrong now?" she asked huskily.

He stopped and looked up. "Wrong? Nothing. I just decided to quit early today and go down to the creek. You weren't there and the car was gone so I thought I'd find you here daydreaming."

He climbed the steps and took her in his arms. She clung to him feeling enormous relief. She said, "Andy; I did something today you won't approve of."

"Bought some chairs?"

"I went out to tell your father what Mister Jamison said he was going to do to all of us."

He led her to the crate, eased her down upon it and sank to the boards beside her. "What did he say?"

"Well, not very much because he was called to the telephone, but he told me not to worry. He said that twice, and Mister Richards was there; he said the same thing."

Andy smiled up at her. "Then you don't have to worry, do you? Charley Prentiss told me all that wild talk Jamison made. Charley said he talked to the County Attorney this morning and was told they'd prosecute Jamison to the limit, so if it's a fight he wants it's beginning to look like he's going to get all he'll want."

"Andy, let's drive out to your father's place."

He arose shaking his head. "Maybe later, Marty. Right now I want a hot bath, then some supper, and then maybe we can sit out here and wait for the moon."

She got up. "We don't have any towels."

He laughed at her expression and went out to his car, brought back a package and herded her inside to open it. There were towels, sheets, pillow-slips, wash-rags and even dish-towels.

"Stopped in town," he explained, and headed for the bathroom with one large white towel. "There's some other stuff out in the car if you want to make dinner," he said, winked at her and closed the door.

She went after the groceries and later, while she was putting them in the cupboards, she had to bite her lip to keep from crying.

She didn't know why she wanted to cry.

It was close to sunset when he came out in fresh clothing and smelling less of wood-sap and more of soap. She went into his arms and hung there. Only the smell of something perilously close to burning made her break away.

They took their plates out onto the porch. He said they'd eventually have to get a table and some chairs for the porch. He asked her if she'd remember to deposit that cheque at the bank. She hadn't; it was still on her dresser at home. But she promised to take care of it the very next day.

She asked how the work had gone and he replied that it had gone so well today he'd quit early on that account. When they finished eating he leaned back, watched the sky a moment then said, "Marty; September's still more than a week off. It's not going to look good, us meeting here every day. Folks'll start to talk." He turned his head and was smiling. "Maybe instead of going out to see my father tonight we'd better go see the minister."

She was appalled. "Tonight . . . !"

He shrugged at her. "Well; how about tomorrow then if tonight's too sudden?"

She slid off the crate into his arms. "Tonight or tomorrow, whatever you wish," she whispered, and sought his lips in the dusk.

"Tomorrow," he said. "I'll come by for you about noon. We'll get married before anyone — "

She silenced him with her fervour, then clung to him in rapturous silence while the sun dropped completely away and long shadows began their steady march up the long yard from the roadway.

Chapter Twenty-Two

He left the details up to her. She was to deposit the cheque first thing in the morning then go make arrangements with the minister. He'd take fuel to his camp in the woods, bring back his laundry, get a haircut and meet her at the little house before noon.

She had so many details to take care of she scarcely knew where to start, but true to her promise she telephoned the Weatherby estate from the bank, got Rachel Moody instead of Mister Weatherby and told her they would be married shortly after noon. Rachel was delighted and promised to tell Andy's father. She also mentioned telling John Richards.

Mike knew; Martha had told him the night before. He had a couple of small drinks at the kitchen sink while she'd been cleaning up the dishes he'd left from getting his own supper. He seemed alternately pleased for her and depressed. By morning he'd evidently come to some kind of compensatory understanding because he was cheerful. Before she'd left to go uptown she'd made him promise to bathe and wear his suit, and to meet them at the church without skirmishing with some bartender on the way.

The minister, a gaunt old man with friendly eyes, was perfectly agreeable, and evidently because he realized how she felt, cautioned calm. Which was of course excellent advice to give. It just wasn't easy advice to follow.

Still, time passed swiftly. There was only one discordant note; as she was hurrying from the church she nearly collided with Mister Jamison, free on bail.

He barred her way, considered her flushed face and said, "It's too bad a pretty girl like you has to always pick losers, Martha."

He'd never used her first name before and she resented him using it now. She would have brushed past, unwilling to talk with him or be delayed, but he stood his ground.

"I know what the hurry's all about. It's the talk of the town. Too bad you have to start your married life with big trouble staring you in the face."

She said sharply, "I wouldn't have to but for you, Mister Jamison. Why are you so bent on making trouble? No one's hurt you."

"Haven't they? What do you call being arrested?"

"You brought that on yourself." She looked into his bleak eyes, pondered throwing herself upon his mercy, decided it would only be a waste of time, and said, "All you're going to do is start something that'll be unpleasant for all of us, and something you're going to regret. If I were you I'd forget the whole thing."

He smiled. "But I can't just forget it. My attorney thinks we've got a good case for damages."

"What would you expect an attorney to tell you, Mister Jamison?" She was angry now and quick with her answers. For some reason she wasn't afraid of him. She had been the day before, terribly afraid, but not today in morning sunlight with the town all around her.

"I'm going to teach those Weatherbys a few things. Before I'm through — "

A thick shadow fell between them. Jamison paused to look. Charley Prentiss had come up silently from behind Jamison. He looked grim and willing. Without taking his eyes off Jamison Charley said, "Marty; is he bothering you?"

She shook her head. "Not really."

Constable Prentiss raised a thick finger, tapped Jamison sharply on the chest and jerked his head. "Shove off," he growled. "Keep away from her. Next time I'll run you in."

Jamison was about to speak but Prentiss's finger poked harder, pushing Jamison off balance. Charley repeated his curt order. Jamison's eyes turned very dark with venom but he turned on his heel and marched away.

Charley let his arm drop and kept watching until the city-man was gone, then he turned and made a heavy smile. "Some guys never learn.

That simpleton doesn't know it yet but he's tangled with a den of tigers."

Martha waited. She knew Charley would explain. He eventually did; he told her Lynne Weatherby's attorney had arrived in town from New York City that very morning, had come round to the jailhouse to read the charges Jamison had been booked on, and had let it be known he was in Carleton to represent anyone Jamison was planning on making trouble for.

"He's one of those quiet ones," said Charley, referring to the lawyer. "One of those high-powered New York fellers who know the law backwards and forwards. Next to Jamison's local attorney he's as sleek as a tiger." Charley shook his head. "I feel sorry for Jamison."

Martha changed the subject; told Prentiss she and Lynne Weatherby's son were to be married in a couple of hours. He was pleased about that, said he'd always liked Andy, that one thing he'd always liked was the way Andy never lorded it over anyone that he was a Weatherby. Then Charley said, "Don't worry, Marty. If Jamison gets in the way I'll be watching. Don't you worry about a thing."

She left Charley Prentiss feeling warm towards the people who were so willing to help. Not only influential people like Mister Weatherby, but people like Charley and old John and even Rachel Moody, and her father. She even forgot about Jamison although she saw him one more time as she hastened back to her father's old car.

He was emerging from his attorney's office and stopped to venomously glower as she climbed into the car and drove off.

There was one thing, though, she didn't quite know how to handle; it had been naggingly present in the rear of all her thoughts since yesterday. She'd mentioned it to no one because it was her personal and private problem: How did a girl who had lived all her life in one house — move out? It didn't seem right, somehow, to simply drive down there, load all her clothes and other effects into the old car and drive away never to return except as her father's guest.

She knew her present mood of quiet rapture would overwhelm the memories long enough for her to make the move, but she also suspected it was going to be very painful going through the physical details of moving.

All her childhood had been spent down there alongside the creek. All her formative years right up until she'd dropped out of high school. That old house in shantytown held all her sorrows, knew all her secrets, had sheltered both her dreams and her innocence. She'd matured there; had found out from observation that people were all different.

She drove to the little house to be briefly alone, but ten minutes later Andy drove in smelling wonderfully of barbershop cologne. He took her out back where sunlight and good earth made their fragrant jungle and held her at arm's length by the shoulders. He was as solemn as a judge when he asked her if she were sure.

"You've got to be positive, Marty."

She *was* positive. She even smiled up at him saying she was confused about a lot of things, but not her love for him. Of that she'd been absolutely positive for a long time.

He pulled her in close. She encircled his chest with both arms. He was a very vital person; handsome and strong and very vital. Whatever else life might hold for her with him, it would never be dull. She squeezed then stepped back and raised up on tiptoes. He kissed her, moving his lips upon her mouth until she brought both hands against his chest and pushed. But he didn't release her. His breath broke hard upon her cheeks, for a little moment panic held her, then she got free and stepped clear. He showed a smoky glance and a soft smile.

She reached to push her hair back into place and said they should get ready. Then, turning squarely to face him, she asked if he had any regrets, any misgivings.

He laughed at her seriousness. "No; and if I'd had any I'd have let you know long before this. Did you remember to put the cheque in the bank?" When she nodded he fished in a pocket and brought forth another cheque. " 'Think you can remember to do the same with this one?"

She took it. The amount was even larger than the first cheque. She raised round eyes. He was looking a little self-satisfied which she could forgive under the circumstances.

"I sold it all. Everything racked up on Jamison's property to a large lodge downriver a few miles that caters to skiing groups all winter long. They burn an awful lot of wood, they told me, and if I had more that would be dry enough later on, they'd buy that too."

She felt the tears coming so looked down at the cheque again. He took her arm and led her towards the house. When she stole an upward glance he was still softly smiling. Well he could feel that way. The cheque was for enough to pay their rent for a long while and to also buy whatever other furniture they would want.

He was dressed adequately except for a dark coat which he had out in the car. While he went for it — and for a little square box he'd hidden from her, along with an even smaller one which he tucked into a pocket — she hastened into the bedroom to make certain her hair was in place when she put on the perky little white hat with its veil. She even had elbow-length gloves. Her father would have recognized both hat and gloves; they had belonged to her mother.

When Andy returned and handed her the larger box she had to bite her lip to keep from crying. It was a small bouquet and squarely in the middle was one dusky rose.

To hide embarrassment Andy went out front to put on his coat, then called to her that he was ready. She came to the door. He looked and said she was very beautiful. She acknowledged the high compliment with a question.

"Have you the ring?"

He tapped a pocket, then went over and bent down for her to softly kiss him. She put out a hand in case he'd grab her. She didn't want to appear rumpled when they got to the little church.

Outside, the sun was slipping slightly off-centre. It wasn't as hot as it had been. There were filmy streamers of transparent clouds forming out over the Pawtucket.

"Rain," she murmured as they got into his car. "Tomorrow maybe."

He paused in the roadway to change gears and looked down. "If it rains tomorrow I won't be able to go up to the woodlot."

She blushed and looked straight ahead.

The town was quiet in its afternoon bath of heat, but when he drove through enough back streets to reach the church there were several cars there including his father's unmistakable Lincoln Continental. Right ahead of it was her father's deplorable old vehicle. Even Charley Prentiss was there in a fresh uniform; despite the heat Charley looked very cool.

She saw Rachel — in her light straw hat — and old John Richards wearing a dark suit and necktie, something she'd never before seen him wear. He didn't look at all comfortable but he looked pleased when he saw her, and lowered his head to speak to Rachel.

She clutched the bouquet in one hand with her other hand on the door-handle. "Andy; do I look all right?"

"No one ever looked better, Marty."

"I mean — do I look upset or anything?"

"Just beautiful," he said, leaning down to brush his lips across her cheek, then open the door for her. "Just beautiful is all."

They stepped over into some tree-shade beside the car. Everyone was watching them now. She thought she'd faint. Andy looked a little peaked too until she said, "You're as scairt as I am," then he braced his shoulders, took several deep breaths and took her free hand to lead her on up where the people were waiting.

"Just not used to this coat is all," he said in a low mutter.

They encountered John and Rachel first. Andy and old John shook hands, held on for a moment longer than was customary, then let go. Old John drawled, "Son; you sure go to a heap of trouble just to get a steady cook."

They grinned at one another.

Rachel kissed Martha and left one little salt-wet tear on her cheek, then straightened up again a proper New Englander.

Charley Prentiss came over to shake with Andy and mumble something that sounded like a congratulation to Martha, but Mike and Lynne Weatherby were talking too, so whatever Charley had said got lost.

Andy's father stood facing his son. The others fell back a step or turned to Martha. For five seconds Martha held her breath then Andy slowly lifted his arm and extended his hand. His father

223